WAR IN THE DESERT

Brondo—Born an Apache, son of the much-feared war chief Cochise, he had a conscience and a heart, and he would defy his own people and the white man's army to bring peace to Arizona—and to win the woman he loved.

Rayva Johnston—She was the adopted daughter of Col. Brett Johnston, commandant of Fort Bowie. A half-breed Apache herself, her beauty caused jealousy and strife among the officer corps and captured an Indian's heart forever.

Red Stoker—One of the most ruthless and vicious outlaws in the history of a lawless territory, he wanted money and would stop at nothing, not even murder, to become the richest and most feared man in the desert.

Betty Wilson—The faithless wife of a loyal army captain, she lied and schemed for love and riches. And when she joined forces with Stoker, she would commit the ultimate betrayal and bring death to many innocent people.

The Stagecoach Series
Ask your bookseller for the books you have missed

STAGECOACH STATION 30:
RAWHIDE

Hank Mitchum

Created by the producers of
**Wagons West, White Indian,
Badge, and Winning the West.**

Book Creations Inc., Canaan, NY · Lyle Kenyon Engel, Founder

BANTAM BOOKS
TORONTO · NEW YORK · LONDON · SYDNEY · AUCKLAND

STAGECOACH STATION 30: RAWHIDE

*A Bantam Book / published by arrangement with
Book Creations, Inc.*

Bantam edition/July 1987

*Produced by Book Creations, Inc.
Lyle Kenyon Engel, Founder*

ISBN 0-553-26571-7

Published simultaneously in the United States and Canada

PRINTED IN THE UNITED STATES OF AMERICA

O   0 9 8 7 6 5 4 3 2 1

STAGECOACH STATION 30:

RAWHIDE

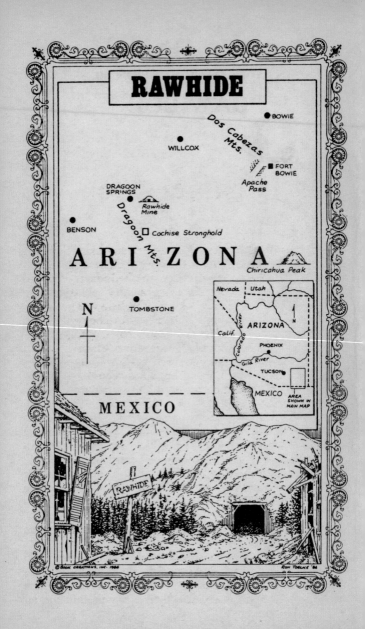

Chapter One

Lightning flashed blue-white against the black thunderheads swirling angrily over the craggy Chiricahua Mountains. Under its glare, a half dozen Apache Indians crouched in the rocks above Fort Bowie's cemetery, observing the somber funeral ceremony taking place below. The leader of the band was a young Chiricahua Apache, whose big Appaloosa, hidden among the nearby trees, stamped nervously beside the pintos of the other five braves.

The accelerating wind plucked at the young leader's long black hair, which lay on his broad shoulders. Adjusting the red headband on his brow, he let his eyes drift to the fort a quarter mile away. For a moment he studied the squat adobe buildings and the surrounding stockade fence, and then he lifted his gaze skyward. The dark, churning clouds held the promise of rain, which southeastern Arizona's wind-pocked and thirsty land would welcome.

The young man returned his gaze to the cemetery below. Watching the scene for a moment, he said to his companions, "Whoever they are burying, it is not a soldier."

Without speaking, the five other Apaches looked at him quizzically.

Responding to their unspoken question, he answered in his basso voice, which was especially deep for his twenty-three years. "When soldiers are buried, seven riflemen stand near the grave and fire their weapons into the air

1

three times in unison, a salute to the memory of a brave soldier. I see no riflemen below."

The five nodded and then turned their dark eyes back to the scene.

The swirling mass of clouds was dropping lower. A jagged bolt of lightning slashed across the sky, followed by a rumble of thunder. In the cemetery Colonel Brett Johnston stood at the foot of the yawning grave, his shoulders drooped. Next to him stood his adopted daughter, Rayva, her black hair draping her beautiful face. The fort's chaplain was reading the Twenty-third Psalm, lifting his voice above the howling wind so as to be heard.

The solemn troops stood at attention surrounding the grave, the wind whipping at their dark blue uniforms. Rayva Johnston's heart felt like hot lead within her breast. The strong arm of her adopted father pressed her close to him as she dabbed at her eyes with a handkerchief. The beautiful raven-haired woman looked from the doleful pine box that sat beside the grave to the wooden cross that had been driven into the ground.

A kind soldier had hastily carved crude letters into the cross:

In Memory of Beloved
Martha Johnston
Feb. 4, 1815—May 11, 1872

The chaplain closed his Bible and offered a brief prayer for those whom Martha Johnston had left behind. He then leaned over and took a handful of dirt from the mound next to the grave while four soldiers lowered the pine coffin with ropes. When the ropes were pulled out and the four uniformed men had stepped back, the chaplain stood at the grave's edge and let the dirt drop from his hand onto the top of the coffin. In a sorrowful monotone he said, "Ashes to ashes, and dust to dust."

The silver-haired colonel left Rayva and gathered his own handful of the dirt. Following the example of the chaplain, he allowed the dry earth to fall into the grave, the wind taking its own share and pelting it against the blue uniforms. Solemnly he said, "Ashes to ashes, and dust to dust."

He stepped back, motioning for Rayva to take her turn, but she shook her head, refusing. Her eyes were misty, but the colonel could see that she was not about to partake of the ritual.

Tiny drops of rain had begun to splatter on the dry, dusty ground, and lightning flashed repeatedly as the colonel slid an arm around the young woman. "Come, Rayva dear," he said softly. "Let's get back to the fort before the rain starts falling hard."

The colonel led his twenty-year-old adopted daughter past two women and several ranks of uniformed men to an army wagon hitched to two horses. The sad eyes of the soldiers and the women showed sympathy for their commandant. One of the women detached herself from the huddle and approached the bereaved father and daughter just as the colonel was about to help Rayva into the wagon. Touching the commandant's arm, the woman said tenderly, "Colonel, all of us loved your Martha. She was a soldier's wife in the truest sense."

Johnston smiled weakly. "Thank you," he breathed.

The woman stepped back, and under the watchful eyes of the mourners, the colonel assisted Rayva into the wagon. As she settled in the seat Johnston circled around the rear of the wagon, heading for the driver's side.

A bolt of lightning suddenly lanced out of the black sky, and thunder cracked loudly above the heads of the horses. The frightened team bolted, throwing Rayva from the seat into the back of the wagon. Colonel Johnston stood stunned, watching the bounding wagon bounce and fishtail across the rugged terrain. His heart turned to ice when he realized that the terrified horses were headed for the edge of a cliff, that the two-hundred-feet-deep chasm was barely half a mile away.

The colonel found his voice as he saw several soldiers running for their horses to take up pursuit. "Hurry!" he shouted. "*Hurry!*"

The soldiers would be too late, and Johnston knew it. The frightened team was blindly racing toward the yawning chasm, obscured by the darkness of the cloud cover.

The colonel saw Rayva struggle to her knees in the wagon bed, falling several times in the process. Lifting her head and looking beyond the team, she must have realized that the horses were headed in a beeline for the chasm, which was coming up fast. The colonel watched in horror as she looked around her at the sharp rocks and clumps of cactus scattered on the ground. From the position she took, it appeared that she was going to jump.

Johnston gasped. Leaping from the speeding wagon could mean serious injury, even death, yet he knew that staying aboard the wagon and going over the cliff with the crazed horses would leave her even less chance of survival. His heart seemed to stop as he watched her crawl laboriously to the side of the wagon bed, readying herself for the jump.

At that instant he saw something appear from behind a jagged rock formation—an Apache riding a huge Appaloosa. Man and horse seemed almost a streak as the muscular animal galloped alongside the wagon.

Rayva was about to jump when the wagon hit a deep rut. The jolt tumbled her back onto the floor of the bed. Hastily, as the dark, hollow canyon came closer, she worked her way back to her knees. Suddenly her attention was drawn to the huge black-and-white Appaloosa pulling up alongside the wagon. From the corner of her eye she caught a glimpse of the galloping soldiers to the rear. The muscular young Apache on the Appaloosa was leaning over, curling his arm toward her.

"Grab hold!" he shouted.

Rain was striking Rayva's face as she strained to keep her balance while reaching toward the strong arm that invited her to safety. The edge of the cliff was only a hundred yards away. But then, as Rayva's hand touched the man's arm, the wagon hit another rut, and she fell back to her knees.

Again the Apache pulled his horse close to the bounding wagon, glancing at the edge of the cliff sweeping toward

him. Gasping with fear, Rayva blinked against the driving
rain and scrambled to the side of the wagon as a white
dagger split the black sky overhead. Rayva could not hear
the answering thunder for the rumble of the wagon and
the pounding of the team's hooves.

The Indian leaned in close, knowing that he had only
one more chance to save the young woman's life. "Jump
into my arm—now!" he shouted.

Rayva Johnston clamped her jaws tight and stood up.
Swaying momentarily, she threw caution aside and lunged
for the Apache's arm.

The strong young man pulled her to him and then, only
inches from the ragged edge, swerved the Appaloosa away
from the cliff, carrying Rayva to safety.

The deranged team was now over the edge, plunging
downward, the wagon trailing after them. The wheels
spun freely while the animals pawed the air with their
hooves. And then horses and vehicle disappeared into the
black abyss.

The Indian reined the Appaloosa to a halt as Rayva
clung to him, her whole body trembling. The mounted
soldiers were approaching at a gallop, with five Apaches
following. The sky flashed and rumbled, and the rain came
down hard.

With the black-haired woman still holding him tightly,
the Indian asked, "Are you all right, miss?"

Gasping, and then glancing fearfully to the spot where
the horses and wagon had plummeted out of sight, Rayva
said, "Yes." When the man turned in the saddle to see her
face, Rayva's arms went around his trunk, and his arms
encircled her in response.

Within seconds more than a dozen blue-uniformed men
pulled to a halt, the five Apache warriors coming to a stop
alongside them.

Lieutenant Gary Donovan slid quickly from his saddle
and darted to the Appaloosa. Wiping rain from his face, he
lifted his hands toward Rayva and said crisply, "I'll take
her now, Indian!"

Rayva trembled and clutched the Apache, still terribly

frightened, her fingernails digging into his flesh. Her face was white, her lips scarlet against the pallor.

Temper rising, Donovan looked at the Indian with smoldering eyes, his mouth a grim downturned line. "I said I'll take her now, Indian!" he snapped heatedly. His hands, still uplifted, were now shaking from his anger.

The Indian looked at the beautiful young woman who was still clinging to him. His color darkened, and a stubbornness formed along the square line of his jaw. Smiling tightly, he said, "I will release her when she is ready."

"I said *now*, Indian!" spat the lieutenant. "She is the colonel's daughter!"

At that instant, Colonel Brett Johnston rode up on a borrowed horse, accompanied by Captain Hale Wilson. As the colonel dismounted, Donovan said to him, "Sir, I have ordered this Indian to release Miss Rayva into my hands, and he refuses to do so!"

Gesturing with a slight wave of his hand, Johnston said calmly, "It's all right, Lieutenant." Stepping close to the Appaloosa, he looked up at the Indian and smiled. "I want to thank you, Apache. I don't know where you came from, but I'm mighty glad you were there. I am Colonel Brett Johnston, of Fort Bowie, and as Lieutenant Donovan told you, the young lady whose life you just saved is my daughter, Rayva. I am in your debt."

Smiling, the Apache looked at the aging army officer with friendly eyes. "The colonel owes me nothing," he said. "Saving the beautiful lady's life was my pleasure."

Gary Donovan gritted his teeth silently.

With a shaky voice Rayva said to the Apache, "I can never thank you enough for what you did. You have my eternal gratitude."

The young man's white teeth gleamed as he gave her a warm smile. "As I just told your father, Miss Rayva, saving your life was my pleasure."

Rayva slid off the Appaloosa into the arms of her father. Two bolts of lightning chased each other across the sky, throwing light on her face. Getting a good look at her, the Apache perceived that she had Indian features, and he wondered why the colonel would have an Indian wife.

While Johnston held his daughter, Lieutenant Gary Donovan approached them and said, "Would you like to ride back to the fort with me, Rayva?"

The colonel looked down, gave her an approving nod, and then released her into Donovan's hands. The lieutenant quickly hoisted her into his saddle. Mounting up behind her, he gave the Apache a smug look.

The wind drove the rain hard against horses and men as more lightning bolts zigzagged across the heavy sky. Thunder boomed like cannon causing some of the horses to nicker nervously.

Lifting his voice above the thunder, Johnston spoke to Donovan. "I want to talk to the Apache for a few moments, Lieutenant. Take Rayva on back to the fort so she can get dried off."

Donovan saluted sharply and nudged his mount toward the fort. As they rode away, Rayva caught the Indian's eye and gave him a fleeting smile.

Colonel Brett Johnston sloshed through the mud, stepped into the stirrup, and swung into his saddle. Under the gaze of his men and the Apaches, he guided his horse close to the big Appaloosa and extended his hand. As the Indian took it in his strong grip, the colonel said, "I want to express my gratitude again for what you did. We just buried Rayva's mother. Rayva's all I have left in the world. If you hadn't saved her, my life would be in shambles now."

"I am sorry about your wife, Colonel," the Indian said solemnly.

"Thank you." Fumbling a bit for words, Johnston said, "Rayva . . . Rayva was right. You have earned our eternal gratitude. I know . . . I know we whites and you Apaches are at odds, son, but for what you did, I consider you a friend." Smiling broadly, the colonel asked, "What is your name?"

Their hands still clasped tightly, the young Apache replied, "I am Brondo, third son of Cochise."

As the last four words filtered into Johnston's mind, the smile drained from his face. Brondo was aware of the enmity between his father and the fort's commandant, and now he could clearly see the hatred for Cochise in the colonel's eyes.

Johnston released Brondo's hand and gave him a stiff salute. Running his bleak gaze over the other five Apaches, he rode away in the driving rain. The other men in blue nodded grimly at Brondo and, goading their mounts, followed their senior officer toward Fort Bowie.

Chapter Two

"**R**each for the ceiling!" roared a redheaded man, shattering the stillness in Tucson's Pima County Bank. The lower part of the outlaw's face was covered with a bandanna, and his hat was pulled low.

Quickly three of gang leader Red Stoker's masked men began to relieve the two tellers of their money. Both of the tellers were men, and their eyes bulged with fear. In front of each window was a customer, one a man, the other a woman. She threw a hand to her mouth, gasping, while the male customer, in his late sixties, blanched white as he lifted his hands.

The sharp crack of Red Stoker's voice brought bank president Nathan Sutter's head up from where he sat at his desk behind the wooden rail and wicket gate.

Holding his revolver cocked and ready, Stoker bellowed, "Any cute tricks, and somebody dies!" His eyes flicked to the bank president and the female bookkeeper, Marian Dokes, who sat near him behind the rail.

As the robber's gaze returned to his men, who were still collecting money from the tellers, Nathan Sutter looked disdainfully at the masked men. His hands were lifted level with his head, fingers twitching.

Marian saw Sutter's eyes drop to the partially open drawer in front of him. The middle-aged woman knew the bank president kept a small-caliber revolver in the drawer. Biting her lips nervously while holding her own hands

9

erect, she looked at Sutter with fearful eyes and shook her head in warning.

Nathan Sutter was about to ignore Marian's warning and go for the gun when Red Stoker's piercing gaze fell on him again. Licking his lips, Sutter froze, sweat beading his brow. Sutter was fifty-eight years of age and wanted to live a long life, but bank robbers infuriated him, and he wanted to shoot them down.

Marian saw this attitude in Sutter's face and moved her lips silently, saying, "There are too many of them!"

"Hurry up, you guys!" Stoker shouted at his men. "We haven't got all day!"

"You want it all, don't you?" snapped Duane Cowger.

"Yeah!"

"Then keep your shirt on! These two gents have shaky fingers, and they keep droppin' money."

Louie Tippett, who held his gun on the other teller, hissed, "C'mon, man . . . get it stuffed in the bag!"

The teller nodded fearfully, doing his best.

Dick Fischer held his gun on the male customer and said, "I want your wallet, mister."

As the man was producing it from an inside coat pocket, Fischer spotted a gold watch chain hanging from the vest pocket. When the frightened man handed him the wallet, Fischer said, "I want the watch and chain, too."

"Aw, please, mister," pleaded the silver-haired customer. "The watch is an heirloom. It belonged to my grandfather."

Fischer's gun barrel came down hard on the man's temple. He fell to the floor, dazed.

The woman customer wailed tremulously, and the outlaw pointed his gun between her eyes and hissed, "Shut up!" Yanking her purse from her trembling hand, he pawed through it, took out the few bills that were inside, and dropped it on the floor. Then he knelt and took the watch and chain from the fallen man, whose head was shaking.

Nathan Sutter desperately wanted to take the gun in his drawer and shoot the robbers down, but Red Stoker was not giving him the opportunity. Stoker shifted his glance toward Sutter often enough to keep the man off balance.

When the teller whom outlaw Duane Cowger held at gunpoint had emptied his cash drawer, Cowger snarled, "Okay, pal, now go get all the money that's back there in the safe."

The teller was wheeling to obey when a fifth outlaw, Bob Deering, burst through the door and said excitedly, "We got trouble, boss!"

Stoker glanced at Deering and said, "What is it?"

"The sheriff and his deputy are headin' this way on the boardwalk! They might be comin' right here to the bank!"

"Come inside and shut the door!" commanded Stoker. "How long we got?"

"Maybe forty seconds!"

Marian Dokes watched the eyes of Nathan Sutter. He was about to go for the gun. "No!" she whispered. "They'll kill us!"

Sutter hesitated. Sweat was running into his eyes.

Stoker said to his men, "We'll have to forget the money in the safe." Looking at the tellers, he barked, "You two! Act like you're takin' care of your customers. You give any warning to the lawmen, we'll kill you. Do you hear?"

Both tellers nodded. Stoker pushed the frightened woman up to the window and jammed her purse into her hand. Cowger jerked the elderly man to his feet, and shoved him up to the window. "Business as usual," he warned.

The redheaded outlaw leader then stepped to the wooden railing and said to the bank's president, "You can drop your hands now. You and sweetie pie here had better play this out good."

Marian swallowed hard.

Sutter lowered his hands, placing palms down on the top of the desk. Furtively he eyed the handle of the revolver in the drawer before him.

Stoker herded his four men toward the front of the bank, where they flattened themselves against the wall. The unsuspecting lawmen would not see them there until they were inside the bank. The outlaws would have the drop on them.

Boots scraped on the boardwalk outside, and the shadows of the two lawmen appeared against the translucent glass of the door. With guns in hand, the gang waited as the two men stood talking in front of the door.

Red Stoker saw that both Duane Cowger and Louie Tippett were holding tightly stuffed money bags. Apparently the gang had done well in spite of not being able to clean out the safe. Stoker looked again toward the door. The knob was now turning. The outlaws stood ready. He saw Nathan Sutter and Marian Dokes stiffen and the tellers look over their customers' shoulders, eyes frozen on the shadows at the glass in the door. Everyone could hear the voices of the lawmen.

The door started to come open, and then it shut again. Someone had come along the boardwalk and was now engaging the lawmen in conversation. Stoker swore. He wanted to get this thing over with. A long minute passed, and the tension continued to build.

Suddenly the door came open. Stoker and his men were ready to give the lawmen a surprise, but instead of sheriff or deputy appearing, a young man in his early twenties entered. It was Marian Dokes's son, Lanny. The instant he closed the door behind him, Stoker clubbed him in the head with his gun barrel. Marian Dokes shrieked as she saw him fold up and slump to the floor.

"Drag him out of the way!" Stoker told his men.

Quickly, Lanny Dokes was dragged into a corner where he would not be seen by the lawmen when they came through the door. Marian began to cry, but Red Stoker pointed a stiff finger at her and whispered a hoarse warning: "Hush it up, lady!"

When Nathan Sutter began rising from his desk to move to Marian, Stoker snapped his fingers loudly. Sutter eased back into his chair, once again eyeing the gun in his drawer.

At that precise moment, the conversation between the lawmen and the person on the street cut off, and they came through the door. Just as the door closed behind them, before Stoker could make a move, Nathan Sutter called out, "Behind you, Sheriff!"

Sheriff Jim Long and Deputy Mike Murrow instinctively clawed for their weapons and whirled about. Five guns roared. Three bullets chewed into the sheriff and two into the deputy.

As the two lawmen went down dead, Marian Dokes screamed, but Nathan Sutter dived into his drawer and came up with the .32 caliber revolver. He began to blast away at the outlaws clustered near the front wall.

Sutter's first bullet ripped into Duane Cowger's rib cage. Guns boomed loudly in the close quarters of the bank as Red Stoker and Louie Tippett unleashed a barrage of shots in Sutter's direction, sending the bank president sprawling over his desk in a bloody heap. Bob Deering shouted at Dick Fischer as he saw one of the tellers bringing a gun to bear from his window. Both outlaws fired, and the two bullets tore into the teller's chest. The customers were trying to leap out of the way as Deering and Fischer fired repeatedly, hitting the other teller. A stray bullet hit Marian Dokes in the head, while another bullet cut down the woman customer. The elderly man panicked. He ran along the nearest wall, crying out unintelligibly. Red Stoker swung his gun around and shot him dead and then turned and shot Lanny Dokes, who was still lying unconscious in the corner.

The bank was filled with blue-white gun smoke. Blinking against its acrid bite, Stoker coughed and said, "Let's get out of here!"

Louie Tippett was kneeling beside Duane Cowger. "Red!" he shouted. "Duane's hit!"

"Help him up!" Stoker said, punching fresh cartridges into his gun.

"I'm hit bad, Red!" shrieked Cowger.

Stoker snapped the cylinder in place, dogged back the hammer, and said without compassion, "Get up, Duane. We gotta go." With that he stepped outside.

Cowger grimaced with pain as Tippett lifted him to his feet. Tippett shoved Cowger's gun into its holster and said, "Throw your arm around my neck, Duane. I'll get you on your horse."

Breathing heavily, Cowger said, "I don't think I can ride, Louie. You'd better leave me here."

"No way, pal," said Tippett. "I'll get you out of here. Come on."

The wounded man hooked his arm around Tippett's neck, and they moved through the door on the heels of the others.

Outside, people were crowding close to the bank. Red Stoker stepped out, waving his gun at them, and snarled, "Get back, everybody!"

The crowd came to an abrupt halt, eyes wide. After a moment a woman screamed. Blue smoke was coming out of the bank's door.

As the outlaws were making their way to their horses, Dick Fischer saw a man come out of a nearby store brandishing a rifle. He shot at the man and hit him in the chest. The man stumbled backward, crashing through the store's large front window. There were more screams.

Red Stoker had just settled in his saddle when a big man came riding up, saw what was happening, and drew his gun. Stoker swung his revolver on him and fired. The man's gun discharged as he buckled and fell from the saddle, and the stray bullet hit a woman in the stomach. She cried out and collapsed.

While the crowd dashed for cover or to attend the three fallen citizens, Louie Tippett hoisted the bleeding Duane Cowger onto his horse and then climbed on his own. The other three men quickly jammed the money bags into Red Stoker's saddlebags, and then the outlaws galloped out of Tucson, heading southeast.

Lester Ainsworth, chairman of Tucson's town council, led a dozen men into the bank. Ainsworth's gaze swept the place. Blood and bodies were everywhere. Some of the men dashed to the two customers, finding them dead. Another looked behind the tellers' cages and saw both of the tellers lying dead.

Ainsworth moved behind the rail, passing through the wicket gate. His stomach flipped over as he saw Marian Dokes lying on her back, a bullet centering her forehead. She lay still, her sightless eyes staring at the ceiling.

Nathan Sutter was sprawled facedown over his desk. He had bled profusely before he died; a pool of blood oozed over the top of the desk.

Ainsworth swore. Turning to face the other men, who were looking over the scene with pale features, he said with determination, "We're not going to let those dirty buzzards get away with this. I'm forming a posse, men. I want nine of you to go with me."

Within fifteen minutes ten angry men were riding out of Tucson on the trail of the Red Stoker gang.

Stoker and his men had pulled the bandannas off their faces and were riding hard toward the town of Benson. Duane Cowger was bent over, barely staying in the saddle. Beside him was Louie Tippett, hand outstretched, trying to keep the injured man from falling. Shouting to Stoker above the rumble of the galloping hooves, he said, "Red! We've got to stop! Duane's in bad shape!"

The red-haired man hollered back, "We can't stop! There'll be a posse on our tails! We gotta keep goin'!"

Tippett's temper flared, but he said no more. He gripped his friend hard, determined not to let him fall. Cowger's head bobbed listlessly, and blood was seeping from his nose and mouth, as well as from the wound in the rib cage. Tippett figured that a lung had been punctured.

The fleeing outlaws had covered only another mile when Tippett lost his grip on Cowger. The bleeding man peeled out of the saddle and hit the ground, cartwheeling. Tippett drew rein, shouting at the others to stop, and bounding from his horse's back, he dashed to Cowger and knelt beside him. The others had turned around and now came to a halt.

Duane Cowger was still breathing but was coughing up blood. Tippett looked up at Stoker, who stayed in the saddle. "He can't ride any more, Red. He's hurt bad."

A sour look formed on Stoker's face. "He has to ride, Louie," he said coldly.

Tippett's face darkened. "I said he can't, Red!"

"We can't leave him behind." An angry tremor made

Stoker's voice rattle. "There'll be a posse. He might be persuaded to talk and identify the rest of us."

Tippett's anger surfaced. His face darkened, and he hissed, "If Duane goes on right now, he'll die!"

Red Stoker's jaw jutted with determination as he drew his revolver, cocked it, and aimed it at Duane Cowger's head. Just as Tippett opened his mouth to protest, Stoker dropped the hammer, the gun bucking in his hand, and a black hole appeared in Cowger's temple.

Smiling wickedly, Stoker said, "The problem is solved now, Louie. C'mon."

Enraged at Red Stoker's cold-blooded murder of Duane Cowger, Tippett slapped leather, going for his gun. Stoker hipped around in the saddle, brought his weapon up, and before Tippett could fire, put a bullet in his heart. The impact of the slug hitting his chest flattened Tippett on the ground.

Holding the smoking gun in his hand, the outlaw ran his eyes over the livid faces of Bob Deering and Dick Fischer. Bitterly, he asked, "Either of you boys upset with me?"

While both shook their heads, Fischer said, "I ain't got no beef with you shootin' Duane."

"Me neither," Deering spoke up quickly. "And as for Louie, he had it comin'. Besides . . . now the bank money will only be divided three ways!"

Red Stoker's ruddy face relaxed, and an imperious smile spread over it as he said, "That's good thinkin', Bob." He chuckled, and then patting his saddlebags where the loot had been stuffed, he said, "We'll divvy it up after we shake that posse. Let's go."

Spurring their mounts, the three men rode hard to the southeast, heading for Benson.

Less than thirty minutes after Duane Cowger and Louie Tippett had been shot dead by Red Stoker, the posse came upon their bodies. Lester Ainsworth, in the lead, raised his hand and drew rein. As the ten riders came to a thundering halt, Ainsworth slid from his saddle and knelt beside the bodies.

"What do you think, Les?" asked Willie Raymond, the town's barber.

Looking over his shoulder, Ainsworth responded, "They're part of the gang, all right. This one with the bullet in his head was the one that came out of the bank shot in his side."

George Keeton, Tucson's blacksmith, leaned from his saddle and studied the tracks leading away from the scene. He spit a brown stream of tobacco juice and said, "Rest of 'em aren't too far away, boys. Those tracks are pretty fresh."

The others agreed. Frank Reardon, one of Tucson's attorneys, said, "From the looks of things, these outlaws aren't getting along very well. Maybe the other three will kill each other off and save us the trouble."

"That would be nice," said Ainsworth evenly. "But until they do, it's up to us to run them down. Let's go."

With renewed determination the posse pressed on.

Ten miles outside of Benson, Red Stoker and his two men pulled into a ravine to rest their horses. While the lathered animals panted for breath Stoker sat down on a large rock, removed his hat, and sleeved away sweat from his brow. When Deering and Fischer sat down beside him, Stoker looked at Fischer and said, "Dick, there's a tree up on the rim of the ravine. Go climb it and take a look-see behind us. I want to know if that posse is comin'."

Fischer bristled at Stoker's order. "Who was your servant this time last year?" he asked curtly. "Go climb the tree yourself."

Bob Deering was surprised at Fischer's rash impudence in the light of what had just happened to Cowger and Tippett. His mouth sagged open.

Stoker looked at Fischer as if he could not believe what he had heard. His eyes burned red-hot. Stoker was not used to being disobeyed, much less being told to do a thing himself. Lines of anger fanned from the corners of his eyes as he snapped, "Are you forgettin' who's boss of this outfit?"

"Look," replied Fischer, "I'm as tired as you are. You may be the boss, but I ain't your slave. I didn't mean no disrespect, but you ain't no better than me. Do some of your own work."

Blood rushed to Stoker's cheeks until they looked raw. "So the boss has to do his own work, huh?"

Fischer shrugged his shoulders. "Things get tough sometimes," he said carelessly. "That's the way the world is."

Stoker whipped out his gun, eared back the hammer, and pointed it between Fischer's eyes. "If that's the way the world is, then you'd be better off out of it, wouldn't you, Dick?" he rasped.

Fischer suddenly realized that he had gone too far. As he looked down the muzzle of Stoker's gun, he thought of Cowger and Tippett lying dead back on the trail. Trepidation showed in his eyes. "N-now, look, Red," he stammered. "I didn't mean—"

Bob Deering spoke up, saying, "I'll go climb the tree, Red."

Holding the gun steady between Fischer's eyes, Stoker grated, "No, you won't, Bob. I told this flap jaw to do it. If he don't, you and I will split the loot *two* ways."

Dick Fischer moved slowly but steadily, rising to his feet. The black muzzle followed his face. "I'll do it," he said shakily. "It's just that . . . well, sometimes I get tired of takin' orders."

Stoker chuckled. "Well, Dick old boy, there's only one way to alter it. You gotta become boss of your own outfit. But if you want to be boss of this one, you gotta kill me. Want to try?"

Shaking his head, Fischer said, "No . . . no, Red. I was just—"

"You was just on your way to climb the tree and look for the posse, right?"

Stoker grinned at Deering and then turned his attention back to Fischer, who was walking toward the tree.

When he had climbed the tree, Fischer squinted against the glare of the desert as it reflected the brilliant sun, studying their back trail for a few moments. Abruptly a cluster of horsemen came into view. They were riding hard, heading directly for them. Scrambling out of the tree, he bounded down the ravine's steep slope. Reaching the bottom, he said breathlessly, "Red, they're comin'! I'd say they're about three miles back."

Stoker swore and spit. Swinging a fist through the air, he said, "I was hopin' we were farther ahead of them. These horses are bushed. But we ain't got no choice. We gotta ride 'em. We'll get fresh ones in Benson." Heading for his horse, he added, "Let's mount up."

"I have a suggestion," Fischer called after him.

Wheeling about, Stoker asked, "What's that?"

"I think we ought to divide up the money right here and now and split up. The posse will have a harder time runnin' us down if we go different directions."

Moving on toward his horse, Stoker said tightly, "Forget it. We're stickin' together. I've got friends at Willcox. We can hole up and hide there till things cool down."

Bob Deering spoke up. "I think Dick's right, Red. We'll be hard to catch if we go different directions. I say we split up."

A wolfish grin twisted Red Stoker's ruddy face, but there was no humor in it. "Okay, boys," he said in a cold monotone, "let's split up." His hand snaked down for his gun, and before Fischer and Deering could react, his weapon belched fire twice. Both men went down.

Stoker swung into his saddle, mumbling, "You boys wanted to split up? Okay . . . we'll split up." Laughing, he spurred his horse out of the ravine and headed for Benson.

Groaning, Bob Deering rolled to his knees. He was gutshot, and he knew there was no way he could live through this—but he would have vengeance on Red Stoker. Rising to his feet unsteadily, he looked down at Dick Fischer. The man was dead.

His body doubled over in pain, Deering laboriously climbed the steep pitch of the ravine. After falling several times, he finally reached the crest, his breath coming in ragged gasps. When his knees gave way, he fell to the ground, and at that moment he heard the rumble of hooves, mingled with the shouting voices of men.

The posse drew up and began to dismount. As Lester Ainsworth stepped to the fallen outlaw, Frank Reardon followed, saying, "Looks like I was right, Les. These guys are killing each other off!"

As Ainsworth knelt down beside him Bob Deering looked up, his eyes turning glassy.

"Where's the other two?" Ainsworth asked, certain that the outlaw was dying.

Licking his lips, Deering groaned and said in a hoarse whisper, "Dick F-Fischer . . . is . . . is at the bottom of . . . of the ravine. Dead. Only . . . one left is . . . Red Stoker. He . . . sh-shot all four of us."

"Where's he headed?" queried Frank Reardon, kneeling beside Ainsworth.

"He's . . . he's goin' through . . . Benson to . . . to Willcox. Has friends at Willcox. They're gonna . . . gonna hide him."

Looking at Reardon, Lester Ainsworth said, "We'll find him if we have to tear Willcox apart."

Reardon nodded, and the rest of the posse joined in agreement. When Ainsworth looked back at the wounded outlaw, he was dead.

Standing up, Ainsworth said, "We don't have time to bury these two either, boys. We'll have to leave their bodies to the buzzards."

"Serves 'em right," said one of the posse.

The others agreed. They mounted up and rode toward Benson. At the livery stable there, they acquired fresh horses—and were told that a redheaded man had just done the same before riding out like the devil was after him. He was not more than ten minutes ahead of them.

Red Stoker pushed his fresh horse hard in a northeasterly direction, heading toward Willcox, Arizona. He was twelve or thirteen miles out of Benson when he topped a rise and glanced behind him. The posse was in view and coming on strong. Stoker swore at the horse beneath him. It was not as fast as he had thought it would be, and the posse was going to catch him.

After riding another mile, Stoker spotted a cluster of huge rocks and boulders up ahead. Glancing behind him and seeing the posse coming out of a draw less than a mile away, he pulled his rifle from the saddleboot and leaped from the saddle, leading the horse between the boulders. Scrambling upward, he settled into a shallow crevice. He had to make a stand, and it was far better to do so here than out in the open. There was a chance the posse would ride on, but even if they did spot him, he could whittle down their number quickly from his protected position in the rocks. Levering a cartridge into the chamber, he waited.

Within seconds the thunder of galloping hooves met his ear, and immediately afterward the ten riders came into view. They were within fifty yards when a band of Apaches suddenly rode out ahead of them from a rock-studded thicket of scrub oak. Two dozen strong, the Apaches opened fire on the surprised posse.

Les Ainsworth's horse reared in fright, spilling him on the ground, and guns boomed all around him as his companions fell one by one under the Apache barrage. Ainsworth lay on his back and pulled his revolver, but he never got to use it. Two Apache bullets ripped into his head.

Red Stoker smiled at the scene from his place of safety. With pleasure he watched the Indians massacre the posse and then jump to the ground with knife blades shining in the sun. He laughed silently as the Apaches scalped their prey.

When the last man's hair was lifted, the Indians mounted up, waving the bloody scalps in triumph. Laughing and shouting with glee, they congratulated each other.

Stoker heard one of the warriors call their leader "Nachise." The outlaw knew Nachise was the eldest son of Cochise, the feared chief of the Chiricahua Apaches, and would one day succeed his father as chief. From what he had just witnessed, Stoker could see that Nachise was as violent and savage as his father. White men would do well to walk a wide circle around him.

Stoker waited until the Apaches had ridden away and passed from sight. Thanking them in his heart for wiping out the posse, he scrambled down the rocks to his horse and rode for Willcox. Dark clouds were filling the Arizona sky as Stoker lashed the horse for its top speed. He wanted to get to Willcox before the rain came.

Chapter Three

A rumbling cannonade of thunder boomed across the rain-soaked desert as Lieutenant Gary Donovan guided his horse through the gate of Fort Bowie.

The corporal who had opened the gate looked quizzically at Donovan and the colonel's daughter and then gazed toward the cemetery.

"The others will be along shortly, Corporal," said the lieutenant. "Miss Rayva had an unfortunate incident take place. I'm taking her to the colonel's quarters so she can dry off and settle her nerves."

The corporal nodded, blinked against the rain, and started to close the gate. He checked himself, however, when he caught sight of the funeral entourage moving toward him through the slanting rain.

Rayva Johnston's knees were still weak when Donovan slid from his horse and helped her down in front of the quarters she shared with her father. Wrapping an arm around her, the lieutenant escorted her to the door. When he began to help her inside, Rayva pulled loose from him and said, "I'll be fine now, Gary. Thank you for bringing me home."

Gripping her firmly by the elbow, Donovan stepped up close. Looking down at her, he said softly, "You are beautiful, even when you're soaking wet."

Rayva remained silent, looking at him, then gently removed her elbow from his fingers. "I've got to get dried off, Gary," she said levelly.

Donovan's mouth turned down. This time he gripped her upper arm. "Rayva," he implored, "why don't you give in to it? You know you're attracted to me. Your father likes me. Everything would be so good if you'd just let down your guard."

A flush of anger reddened Rayva's prominent cheekbones. "You mustn't push me, Gary," she said, her lips forming a thin line.

The look in her eyes froze Donovan, and the words he was about to speak died in his throat. He sighed deeply and released her arm. Shaking his head, he walked away in the rain that was beating against the porch roof overhead.

Rayva closed the door and went to her room. Upon entering, she lit a lantern and then proceeded to remove her wet clothing, catching a glimpse of herself in the mirror above her dresser as she did. Her long, coal-black hair was matted to her head, her smooth, creamy complexion streaked and dirty. With her dress partially unbuttoned, she stepped up close to the mirror, thinking, *Rayva Johnston, you'd be dead now if it weren't for that handsome young Apache. What was it you felt when he held you so tight? You've never had that feeling before. . . .*

A cold chill shuddered through her body. Turning from the mirror, she pulled off the wet dress, spreading it over the back of the chair. Even her petticoats were drenched. At that moment she heard the front door of their quarters open and then close. Heavy feet moved toward her door.

The beautiful young woman dashed across the room, pulled a long robe from her closet, and wrapped it around her.

"Rayva?" came her father's voice through the door. "Are you all right?"

"Oh, yes, Father," she called back with relief. "You may come in."

The hinges squeaked as the door opened. Colonel Brett Johnston stood framed in the doorway, looking tenderly at his adopted daughter. "That was an awful close call, honey," he said. "Are you sure you're okay?"

She forced a smile for him, but it did not reach her eyes. "My knees are still a little weak, Father," she replied delicately. "But other than that—"

The colonel reached his adopted daughter in two strides, folding her into his arms. As she wrapped her own arms around his waist she began to weep. After trying to comfort her, he said with a shaky voice, "It would have been more than I could bear if I had lost you today, honey. Losing your mother has crushed me terribly, and if you had gone over that cliff, I—"

Struggling to find her voice, Rayva choked, "It's all right, Father. You still have me."

Father and daughter stood in the middle of the room, the rain beating on the roof, and wept together as they talked of Martha and of how much they would miss her. When their tears had ended, they still clung to each other.

"You are all I have in the world now, honey," the colonel said tenderly. "We must stay close to each other."

"We will, Father," Rayva assured him.

Still holding her tight, he said, "I hope you and Gary will let your friendship develop into a courtship, honey. Nothing would make me happier than to see the two of you marry."

Rayva felt a shiver run up her spine.

Johnston continued, "I'll use my influence with the army to keep Gary assigned to Fort Bowie. That way you'll never be too far from me."

Her head flat against her father's chest, the brunette woman asked, "But what about when you retire, Father?"

"My retirement is nearly two years away, honey," he said softly. "I haven't told you, but I've been doing some thinking."

"Mmm-hmm?"

"I can get Gary assigned here permanently. I could buy a small house in Bowie, and then I'd be close to you—and to my grandchildren as they come along."

Still holding her head against her father's chest, Rayva bit her lip, struggling with her emotions. Lieutenant Gary Donovan was the apple of the colonel's eye, and consequently when Donovan had begun to show serious interest in Rayva, Johnston had encouraged the relationship. Several young soldiers at the fort had attempted to court her, but the only time the colonel had really approved was when Donovan had taken an interest.

Rayva could accept Donovan as a friend, but she had recently realized he was just not what she wanted in a man. The thought of him as a husband had become repugnant to her. However, she had not yet told her father how she felt.

She bit down on her lip, keeping her face from the colonel's view. She wanted to tell him, but she couldn't right now. He had just buried his wife of thirty-nine years and didn't need anything else to upset him.

Changing the subject, Rayva said, "Father, I need to bathe. Would you order me some hot water?"

Johnston kissed his adopted daughter's forehead, patted her cheek, and replied, "Certainly, my dear. I'll have Corporal Smithers bring it right away."

Taking hold of his hand, Rayva lifted it to her lips and kissed it. Looking up into his pale blue eyes, she said, "I love you, Father. You've always been so good to me."

Cupping her lovely face in his hands, he studied the smudges of dirt and said, "I remember seeing your face like this when you were a little girl." Chuckling, he added, "I guess you will always be my little girl."

They embraced one more time, and the colonel stepped to the door. Opening it, he called across the parade ground to one of the men, telling him to send Corporal Smithers. When the order was acknowledged, he turned back and closed the door.

Looking up at the stately man, Rayva said, "Father, I want to thank that Apache more adequately once my emotions have settled down from . . . from Mother's death."

Johnston bristled, and he said bluntly, "I thanked him sufficiently for you. No more is needed."

Rayva looked at him, surprised at his sudden curtness. It was not like him to speak to her in this manner. "Father . . . what's wrong?"

With a deep antagonism, Johnston snapped, "I need

explain nothing to you. I'm your father, and I told you that I thanked the Apache sufficiently. Let the matter drop."

Rayva's brow furrowed, and with misty eyes she said, "But Father, he could have been killed! He risked his life to save me! If it weren't for him, I would have died at the bottom of that cliff."

A stern look in his eyes, the silver-haired colonel said, "I repeat, Rayva, the Apache has been sufficiently thanked. You are not to see him again."

"But Father," she protested, "I heard you tell him that you are in his debt. Certainly you must allow me to—"

There was ice in the colonel's eyes as he rasped, "You are not to see him again!" With agitation written all over his face, he said sharply, "Are you forgetting that this fort is here because we are at war with the Apaches?"

Rayva bristled as she felt the heat of anger wash over her. "Are you forgetting that I am half Apache?" she snapped back.

The colonel's face flushed as he retorted, "You're also half white!"

"I am half white only because a white man sired me when he ravished my Apache mother!"

"May I remind you, young lady, that the Apaches abandoned you *because* you were half white?" Johnston retorted, his words brittle. "If Martha and I had not taken you in after your mother died, you would have starved to death out there in the desert!"

Rayva opened her mouth to speak, but there was a knock at the door, and the colonel turned and opened it. A skinny corporal stood there, wide-eyed and ready for his orders. "You wanted to see me, sir?" he asked.

"Oh, uh, yes, Smithers," Johnston said, nodding. "Miss Rayva wants to bathe. Would you bring her some hot water?"

Briefly shifting his eyes past the commandant to the black-haired woman, Smithers looked at the colonel again and said, "Certainly, sir. I'll have it here within fifteen minutes."

Johnston thanked him and closed the door. When he turned around, he saw Rayva's dark eyes about to spill over with tears. The sight of her tears melted his heart. "Aw, honey," he said, pulling her to himself, "we shouldn't be arguing. We just buried Martha."

Rayva clung to the tall, elderly man and wept silently. She was grieved over the loss of her adoptive mother, but she was also thinking of the handsome young Apache who had saved her life. She wanted to see him again, and her father's angry insistence that she was not to do so tore at her already broken heart. Rayva could not understand why her father would so vehemently oppose her seeing the man who had saved her life. He had fought Apaches for years, but the only one toward whom he had ever shown a burning hatred was the Chiricahua chief, Cochise. Why did he feel so strongly against the young warrior who had spared her a violent death?

Rayva decided to say no more about the Apache for the moment. She would let things settle down. When their grief over Martha's death began to abate, she would find a way to get her father's permission to look up the man who had saved her life and thank him properly.

Father and daughter talked quietly of the funeral service and soon were interrupted by Corporal Smithers, who appeared with two buckets of steaming hot water. As soon as Smithers was gone, the colonel left her quarters, and Rayva bathed in the privacy of her room.

After the funeral cortege broke up inside the fort, Captain Hale Wilson turned his horse over to a trooper at the stable and sloshed through the mud toward his quarters.

Hale, a tall, well-built, handsome man in his mid-thirties, had dark brown hair and wore a neatly trimmed mustache. As he neared the door of his quarters, the irritation within him surfaced. He was perturbed at his wife, Betty, who had refused to attend Martha Johnston's funeral. Betty was beautiful and blond, with a figure that made her the envy of women wherever she went. But her beauty was also a source of strife in their marriage, for men were attracted to her like flies to honey . . . and she loved it.

The captain stepped up on the porch, glad to get out of

the driving rain, and wiped his boots on a gunnysack that lay in front of the door. He opened the door, moved inside, and closed it behind him. At the same moment, he heard a strange shuffling sound from the rear of their quarters, followed by a dull thump.

As Hale was shaking water from his hat, Betty emerged from the shadows at the rear. His heart leaped as he took in her exquisite beauty. She had done her hair in an upsweep with long, tubular curls in the back and tiny ringlets adorning her forehead. She knew this was his favorite style for her hair. Though Hale Wilson frequently grew angry with Betty, she knew how to turn on the charm and make him putty in her hands.

With an infectious smile, the captivating blond woman dashed to him, throwing her arms upward, ready to embrace him. Holding her at arm's length, he tossed his hat on a nearby table, and said, "Betty, I'm drenched. You'll get yourself all wet."

Giggling in her girlish way, she pushed past his hands and wrapped her arms around his neck. "It doesn't matter if I get wet, darling," she cooed. "You're my husband, and I love you. I'll hug you even when you're wet!"

But Hale did not fold her into his arms. She could feel the stiffness in his body and the air of aloofness around him. Easing back far enough to look up into his dripping face, she pressed her full lips into a pout and said seductively, "Is my big man angry with me for not going to the funeral?"

Hale's dark brown eyes settled harshly on hers, and stiffly he said, "Betty, it was not just anybody's funeral. It was Martha Johnston's. I am second in command at this post, and my commanding officer's wife died. It is only common courtesy that his captain's wife be present at the funeral."

Holding his gaze, she asked, "You did tell the colonel and Rayva that I had an awful headache, didn't you?"

"Yes," he replied in a dull tone. "I lied for you like I've done so many times before."

Pushing away from him, Betty turned around and folded her arms over her chest. Still pouting, she said, "Hale, you know how I detest funerals. They leave me with a morbid feeling that takes weeks to shake."

Hale Wilson stood there studying the tubular curls at the back of her head. He loved this gorgeous creature with every fiber of his being—and wished with all his heart that she had turned out to be the loving and faithful wife he had thought he was getting. She had been a sore disappointment in that regard, yet his fiery passion for her made him cling to the hope that she would change. He could be so happy loving her . . . if only she would be the woman he had thought she was when he married her.

But at the moment he was perturbed. "So, you detest funerals," he said flatly. "I don't know anybody who likes them. But they are necessary. People do die. There are some things in life, my dear, that we have to do, even if they're inconvenient or unpleasant."

Betty kept her back to the tall man, saying nothing.

Hale continued, "As the wife of Fort Bowie's captain, Betty, you have a duty to support your husband's position."

Turning her head slightly so as to speak over her shoulder, she rasped, "*I* didn't join the army, Hale, and I don't wear a uniform. I have no responsibility toward the army at all. I married you, not Uncle Sam."

"But I *am* in the army, Betty," he snapped back. "It's my life and my career. A wife is supposed to be a help to her husband. She surely shouldn't do anything to blight his status in his chosen line of work."

Wheeling to face him, Betty widened her eyes and said, "Oh, come on, Hale! Don't tell me that just because I didn't attend that gruesome funeral your status as captain of Fort Bowie has been blighted!"

"No, it's not just that," he responded with a bitter edge in his words. "By far the most damaging thing you have done is to flaunt yourself before the men of this fort. You're far too friendly with them."

Betty's powdered cheeks crimsoned with rage. "You're just jealous! That's what's the matter with you!"

"All right," he half growled. "I am jealous, and I admit it! But more than jealousy, I feel a kind of shame."

"Shame?" she bit back. "What shame?"

Hale's eyes were stormy. "The shame of you making a fool of yourself with your flirtations! The shame of being a laughingstock among the men! It's being whispered all over this fort that the captain should be able to control his wife."

Betty Wilson felt a hot surge of anger flare up within her, but she suppressed it. Now was not the time to have a big fight with her husband. Forcing the fire from her eyes, she pressed her lips once again into a pout and moved slowly to the tall figure. Wrapping her arms around his neck, she placed her full red lips close to his and let him feel her warm breath on his face as she said alluringly, "I can't help it if men find me attractive. Would you want your wife to be homely?"

The deep blue eyes that looked up at him had a cooling effect on Hale Wilson's anger. Gripping her with passion, he breathed, "I want you just like you are, Betty, the most beautiful, captivating female on the face of this earth. But I want you for myself—totally. You are *my* wife!"

Betty threw her head back and smiled. With a finger, she traced a line across his forehead from one temple to the other. "But Captain, you wouldn't want your wife to be rude to the men under your command, would you? It would damage your status if your wife was cold toward them. She must be . . . amiable."

Still holding her tight, Hale said, "You are more than amiable, Betty. Especially with lieutenants Canady and Murdock."

Her eyes fluttered. "Well . . . I—"

"There'll be no more of it, do you hear?" he said, squeezing her tighter.

"I hear," she breathed sweetly.

Hale started to speak again, but she suffocated his first word with a passionate kiss. As she held her lips to his, Betty felt her husband melt under her spell. No matter how angry he got at her, she could ultimately collapse his defenses with her power.

Captain Hale Wilson kissed his wife repeatedly, drowning his doubts of her in his love. Everyone at Fort Bowie knew that Hale was tortured with jealousy and that Betty was leading him on a merry chase. If things did not change, she would destroy him . . . like a disease in his blood or a fever in his soul. He would go on loving her, desiring her, worshiping her, no matter how many times she wounded his heart.

Finally he released her and said, "I need to get into some dry clothes."

Betty turned from him and sat down in an overstuffed chair as he walked into the bedroom, removing his tunic. Raindrops merged into a glistening cascade down the bedroom window. As the captain hung the wet tunic on the back of a straight-backed chair, something caught his eye—water on the windowsill. For some reason the window had been opened and shut while the rain was falling.

Suddenly he remembered the strange shuffling sound and the dull thump that he had heard upon entering their quarters. Feeling a coldness in his stomach, he stepped to the window and pulled it open. There were boot tracks in the mud leading away from the window.

Swearing under his breath, he closed the window. The coldness within him was being replaced by a fury that flowed through his system like molten lava.

Pivoting in a jerky manner, the captain stomped through the bedroom door to where Betty was sitting in the front room. She saw the anger in his face but looked up and smiled innocently.

Blood flushed the sides of his muscular neck. Towering over her, he demanded, "Who was it?"

"What are you talking about?" Betty asked, looking up but not quite meeting his gaze. Feigned innocence framed her lovely features.

"Don't put on that act for me, Betty! Who was it?"

Still wearing a facade of innocence, she said, "Hale, what on earth—?"

"There's water on the windowsill in the bedroom, Betty!" he raged, pointing in that direction.

"Oh," she said sweetly, "I was fixing my hair back there, and the room got rather stuffy. So I opened the window. I just closed it when I heard you come in."

"You're lying!" he blared. "Somebody was back there

with you! I heard him leave when I came in. I also heard
you shut the window behind him!"

"Hale, I—"

"Don't lie, Betty! There are tracks in the mud leading
away from the window!"

Betty could no longer keep the guilt from her face. She
was trying to think of something to say when Hale continued, "It couldn't have been Canady. He was at the funeral. But Murdock was one of the officers on duty inside
the fort while the rest of us were at the cemetery. It was
Murdock, wasn't it?"

Betty dropped her guilty gaze and looked at the floor.
She did not answer.

Hale Wilson's anger increased at her silence. With mounting intensity, he said, "I asked you a question, Betty! Was
it Murdock?"

The beautiful blond woman remained silent.

"Or have you added another boyfriend?"

Without looking up, Betty said glumly, "It was Murdock.
We were only talking."

The irate husband stood like a statue for a long moment,
glaring furiously at his wife. His breathing was ragged,
like that of an angry, wounded beast. Suddenly he turned
and charged out into the pounding rain, leaving the door
wide open.

Chapter Four

Lieutenant Clifford Murdock sat at a table in the unmarried officers' quarters, playing poker with lieutenants
Gary Donovan and Douglas Canady.

Murdock, in his late twenties, stood just under six feet
and was stockily built. He was known to be rugged and
quite capable with his fists. Smoke from the cigarillo between his teeth burned his eyes as he shuffled the cards.
His mind was on the few moments he had spent with
Betty Wilson earlier, and he reveled in the thought of her
sweet lips.

As Murdock dealt a fresh hand to himself and his two
companions, Doug Canady looked at Donovan and said, "I
bet Rayva will see the edge of that cliff coming at her in
her nightmares for years to come."

"A mighty close call," added Donovan, picking up his
cards. Known for his temper, he had light brown hair and
fair skin and was of medium height and build.

Canady said, "Looks like you might have a rival in that
long-haired Apache, Gary."

Donovan's face crimsoned slightly at Canady's words.
He picked up the smoking cigarillo that he had laid in an
ashtray and stuck it in the corner of his mouth. "You mean
just because he risked his dirty red skin to save her life?"

"You know that's not what I mean," Canady responded,
aware of the flush in Donovan's face. "She hung on to him

like he was her knight in shining armor . . . like maybe he was the man she's been waiting for all along."

"From what I hear," put in Clifford Murdock, "it *was* a mighty daring rescue. Wish I could've seen it."

Canady adjusted his lean frame on the chair and said, "It was a genuine hair-raiser, I'm here to tell you that."

Aware of Gary Donovan's romantic intentions toward the colonel's daughter, Murdock picked up the cards he had dealt himself and, looking at Donovan from the tops of his eyes, said, "So this Apache is stealing your thunder, huh?"

Donovan's features darkened. "Rayva was in a real state of fright after this Brondo, I think that's his name, pulled her out of the wagon. She was clinging to him only because she was scared."

Lightning slashed the ebony sky outside, followed by a sharp clap of thunder as the rain continued to soak the desert. Using matchsticks as stakes, the three men made their bets, eyeing their cards through a cloud of smoke.

"Yeah," said Canady. "His name's Brondo." Chuckling, he added, "You guys should've seen the change come over Johnston's face when that Indian told him he was Cochise's son."

Murdock gave a mirthless laugh. "I can picture it. There isn't a bone in Cochise's body that the colonel doesn't hate."

"That's putting it mildly," remarked Gary Donovan. "Those two have faced each other through a lot of gun smoke. Cochise has been a thorn in the old man's flesh for a long time."

"Remember that battle over at Wildhorse Mountain two years ago?" asked Murdock.

"Oh, yeah," responded Canady. "That was when we'd shot it out with about a hundred Apaches. We lost over twenty good men. The sun was going down, and both sides knew the fighting would have to stop. The Apaches drew back into the rocks, and we picked up our dead, about to leave, when we couldn't find Harry Pemberton."

"Mmmph!" grunted Donovan. "Then ol' Cochise appeared up on a ridge on his horse, holding Pemberton's scalp for Johnston to see."

Murdock shook his head, rearranging the cards in his hand. "Whew! The colonel called Cochise every name in the book, then made up enough new names to fill another book!"

"That sure made Johnston hate Cochise," said Gary Donovan, "and the incident last December made it even worse."

"You mean that three-day scrap at the San Simon River?" asked Canady.

"That's the one." Donovan nodded.

The three lieutenants discussed the bloody battle that Colonel Brett Johnston had led against Cochise's Chiricahuas along the banks of the San Simon River some twenty miles north of Fort Bowie. The colonel and a squad of forty men had followed Cochise and his warriors up the river with the intent of capturing the venerable chief and bringing him to trial for murdering white settlers.

Cochise had eluded them the first day of the chase. Johnston and his men had camped along the west bank of the San Simon that night with four sentries posted. When dawn came, all four sentries were gone.

Enraged, Johnston had led his men in search of the Apaches all day but could not find them. That night, camping on the bank of the river, Johnston had posted a double guard of eight men. At dawn, all eight sentries had disappeared. The colonel had blood in his eye that day as he led his men in search of Cochise. The Apaches had crisscrossed the river several times and always stayed ahead of the men in blue.

On the third night, eight new sentries were posted. The men had just settled down for the night when one of the sentries noticed dark objects floating downstream. Thinking the objects were Apaches, floating silently down the river for a night attack, he quietly alerted the colonel.

Under Johnston's orders, the soldiers flattened themselves on the riverbank, ready to open fire on the Indians. When the dark objects drew close, the soldiers found them to be the bodies of the twelve missing sentries, tied to large pieces of driftwood to keep them afloat. Cochise had captured them, cut out their tongues, and tortured them, finally driving wooden stakes through their hearts.

Johnston had almost gone out of his mind with fury. Cochise was nowhere to be found the next day, having somehow slipped away from them and returned to his stronghold in the Dragoon Mountains.

In his rage, Johnston had taken his reduced ranks back to Fort Bowie for reinforcements, ordering every soldier at the fort to arm himself to the teeth for an all-out attack on Cochise's lair. The men knew it would be nothing short of suicide; the Apaches were hidden and protected in the Dragoons so well that any soldiers trying to enter would be wiped out.

Captain Hale Wilson was finally able to talk sense to Johnston, and the suicide mission was called off. But his hatred for Cochise grew. The men in Fort Bowie were well aware of the colonel's feelings toward the Chiricahua chief, and they were not surprised at his change in attitude toward the young Apache who had saved Rayva's life upon learning that he was a son of the despised Cochise.

While the rain continued to beat on the roof, the three soldiers played their hands. Murdock laughed in triumph as he raked the pile of matchsticks toward himself from the center of the table. "Your turn to deal, Doug," he said to Canady.

Doug Canady took the deck and began to shuffle the cards. Then, continuing with the subject of Cochise and the Apaches, Canady said, "From what I'm hearing, Cochise's oldest son, Nachise, is a chip off the old block."

"What do you mean?" asked Gary Donovan.

"I mean Nachise is as mean and savage as his old man. He hates whites with a purple passion and loves to lift their scalps."

"Oh, yeah." Donovan nodded. "I heard about some settlers attacked by Nachise and some of his gang a few weeks ago. Tortured them unmercifully before he killed them."

"Come to think of it," put in Clifford Murdock, "I've heard that Cochise has three sons and that the third doesn't go along with his old man's barbaric ways. In fact, now that I think of it, whoever told me about it said that the third son has urged Cochise to make peace with the whites and put a stop to the bloodshed."

The other two nodded as Murdock filled his lungs full of smoke from the cigarillo and went on. "Seems from what you boys have told me about this Brondo and how he risked his life to save Rayva, he must be that son."

"Sure wouldn't be that second son, Naiche," commented Gary Donovan. "I hear tell he's as mean as his pa and older brother."

Murdock coughed and said, "That's right. I've heard the same thing."

"Well," said Doug Canady, "Brondo sure had no way of knowing that Rayva is half Apache when he took off after the runaway wagon. As far as he knew, he was rescuing a white woman. Any Apache who is totally loyal to Cochise would have let her die—and laughed when it happened."

"That's true," agreed Donovan, "but even if Brondo is not in total agreement with his old man, he's still Cochise's son. That's enough for the colonel to keep him from ever seeing Rayva again."

"So you still have clear sailing, huh?" chortled Murdock.

"Brondo couldn't come between me and Rayva anyhow," murmured Donovan. "He isn't—"

Gary Donovan's words were cut short by the sudden entrance of Captain Hale Wilson, dripping wet. Hale stood there, his tall, broad-shouldered form silhouetted against the falling rain behind him. The three poker players could plainly see that the captain's features were twisted with fury.

Blinking against the water running into his eyes, Hale set his venomous glare on the men and hissed through his teeth, "Murdock, I want to see you in private."

Doug Canady laid down his cards, saying, "Lieutenant Donovan and I will vacate the premises, Captain. You two can talk right here."

Donovan laid down his cards and started to get up.

"No," Hale responded. "You men stay put. Mr. Murdock and I will talk outside."

Canady and Donovan looked at each other and then settled into their chairs. Clifford Murdock sighed, flopped his cards facedown on the table, and stood up. He knew what was coming. Shoving his chair back, he moved toward the captain, meeting his hot glare and then stepping past him onto the barracks porch. The cigarillo was still clamped between his teeth. Following him, Hale Wilson slammed the door.

When the door banged shut, Donovan shook his head and said to Canady, "If the captain doesn't put his wife in tow, he's going to have to whip half the men in this fort."

Doug Canady nodded in agreement. "I don't think he'll ever tame her. The woman has too much of the wild life in her past. Too bad. She'll ruin his chances of becoming commandant when the colonel retires."

"You must not feel too bad about it." Donovan grinned.

Raising his eyebrows, Canady said, "What's that supposed to mean?"

"Oh, come now, Lieutenant," replied Donovan, still grinning. "I'm not blind. You've had that blonde in your arms before."

Flushing slightly, Canady said, "She's got velvet lips, ol' buddy. A man would be a fool to pass them up when they're practically shoved into his face."

"Apparently the captain doesn't know about you, huh?"

Canady cleared his throat. "Well, Betty told me that he suspects we're pretty friendly. But I guess he's waiting for proof."

"You'd better hope he doesn't get it. Because if he does, he'll be after you next."

Canady wiped a nervous hand over his face as Donovan continued, "The captain is a tough cookie, ol' buddy. You think you can take him if he comes after you?"

Shaking his head, the thin lieutenant said, "Not a chance. And I'll tell you what. Tough as Murdock is, he isn't going to take the captain, either. Wilson's going to make mincemeat of him."

Outside, Hale Wilson fixed baleful eyes on Clifford Murdock. He pictured this man holding Betty in his arms, and an angry buzzing reverberated through his head.

Murdock put an innocent look on his face and asked, "What's this all about, Captain?"

"Betty!" Hale steamed.

Murdock hunched his shoulders and started to speak.

"Don't bother to deny it," the angry captain said levelly. "She already admitted it was you."

Murdock felt his blood turn cold and his temples begin to throb. Squaring his thick shoulders, he said through tight lips, "What now?"

With a toss of his head, Hale growled, "We're going to settle this problem out behind the stable." His eyes had the look of a hungry predator.

Clifford Murdock had grown up fistfighting. He had done much of it in the army, building a reputation of being plenty tough. But though he outweighed Hale by thirty pounds, he had no desire to fight with him. He had once seen the captain kill a big husky Apache with his bare hands—and the Apache had not touched Hale Wilson's wife.

Murdock felt a cold hand grip his spine with icy fingers. Hitching nervously at his belt, he said, "Captain, I am not about to strike a superior officer."

Hale Wilson had removed his captain's bars while storming toward the barracks. They were in his pocket. Pointing a finger at his shoulders, he said, "You'll notice I'm not wearing my bars. This little problem is not between a captain and a lieutenant. I am an angry husband who is about to teach a lesson to a dirty snake in the grass who has invaded my home and marriage!"

"Now just a minute, Captain," argued Murdock, straightening his back as if his dignity had just been trampled on. "I was invited through that door! I didn't break it down."

Hissing through clenched teeth, Hale said, "You are about to learn not to go near the door!"

Raising his hands palms up, Murdock choked, "Look, Captain, I want to apologize. Okay? I was wrong. Betty is a beautiful woman, and I simply responded to an invitation. And I—"

"What do you mean *an* invitation?" Hale blurted. "This isn't the first time you've been around my wife!"

Clifford Murdock knew it was too late for apologies. He shrugged his wide shoulders and said, "Okay, Captain. I guess there is no way around this. We might as well get it over with."

"You're dead right there's no way around it, mister! blared the angry husband. "Let's go!"

The men in blue that were scattered along the parade ground under porches and canopies watched the two officers plod through the mud in the driving rain and disappear between two buildings. They wanted to follow and see the fight, but they knew better than to do so.

Hale and Murdock reached the stable and approached the corral. As they drew up to the pole fence, Hale looked around to see if anyone was watching, and satisfied that they were alone, he said, "Climb through the poles, mister. You're going to get your lesson inside the corral."

Murdock blinked against the rain in his eyes, licked his heavy lips, and said, "I'm not fighting you in that muck!"

Fury rankled Hale, and moving with the speed of a diamondback rattler, he seized Murdock's thick frame in a steellike grip, lifted him off the muddy ground, and hurled him over the top rail of the pole fence. While Murdock was rolling in the mud and wet manure, Hale vaulted the fence and went after him like a vulture goes after a piece of bloody meat.

Murdock wiped rain from his face as he scrambled to his feet to meet the angry captain's onslaught. Making a fist, he swung hard, aiming for Hale's jaw, but his feet slipped in the muck, and he started down. Hale hastened in and brought up a knee, catching Murdock square in the face. The lieutenant flopped backward and rolled in the muck.

Towering over him like a murderous giant, the captain shouted, "Get up, Murdock!"

The lieutenant worked his way to his feet once again, clenching both fists. When the captain moved in, Murdock planted his feet more solidly and started swinging. Hale caught a solid right on the side of his head, rocking him momentarily but doing no damage. He let the heavier man throw one more punch, which he ducked, and then drove a quick left to the nose, followed with a savage right to the midsection.

The lieutenant grunted as breath whooshed from his mouth, and he doubled forward. Hale caught him with a stinging right to the left ear. Murdock staggered but righted himself and threw a wild right hook, which connected with Hale's jaw. The blow sent the captain reeling backward, his feet going out from under him as he splashed into the mud and manure.

Murdock was pleased with himself, and with confidence rising, he dashed in as soon as the captain was on his feet. Hale bobbed and weaved, making Murdock miss with another wild punch. In the next instant Hale nailed the lieutenant with a stiff blow to the jaw. Murdock staggered from its impact, and Hale followed with another hard punch to the midsection and a piston-style punch to the point of Murdock's chin. The thick-bodied man went down again.

The horses penned up in the corral were gathered under a makeshift shelter against the driving rain. The sight of the two battling men made them prance about nervously, some nickering.

Clifford Murdock gained his feet again, shaking his head. The last punch had addled his brain. Hale came after him, but then the captain slipped slightly, and Murdock, whose feet were well planted, sent out a punch. Hale felt the shock of the lieutenant's fist as it slammed him squarely on the jaw. His feet lifted out of the muck, and he found himself lying on his back.

Again, Murdock gained some confidence. But it was short-lived.

At that moment Hale Wilson saw flash through his mind a picture of Betty in the arms of this mud-and-manure-covered man. The picture was enough to clear his brain and put fresh fire in his veins.

The angry captain bounded up and met Murdock with a barrage of punches, knocking Murdock's head right and left repeatedly. The lieutenant finally was able to avoid a couple of punches and throw one of his own, which connected with Hale's temple but didn't seem to slow him.

The captain slammed Murdock several times violently, knocking him down once again. As the lieutenant rolled from his back to his stomach, Hale pounced on him, flattening him in the muck. Straddling him and sinking his fingers into Murdock's hair, he snapped his head back and hissed, "You stay away from my wife, do you hear me?"

Closing his eyes against the pelting rain, the lieutenant gasped, "Yes!"

"If you ever go near her again, mister," grated Hale, "you'll think what we're doing now is a children's game. Do you understand?"

Murdock's hair felt as if it were going to come out at the roots. Gritting his teeth against the pain, he shouted, "Yes!"

Still venting his anger, Hale repeatedly mashed Murdock's face into a large pile of wet horse droppings. Then he hoisted the lieutenant to his feet and backed him up against the pole fence.

Murdock was spitting and gasping as Hale braced him up against the fence. The captain planted his feet firmly, and clenching his right fist, he drew it back and unleashed a murderous blow on the man's jaw. Murdock's head whipped sideways from the impact and then rebounded. Hale struck him again with the same kind of blow and stepped back. The lieutenant teetered momentarily and then toppled into the muddy slime.

Betty Wilson sat in the overstuffed chair and watched the slanted wall of rain that closed behind her irate husband after he stormed out of their house to find Cliff Murdock. Swearing to herself, she rose from the chair and closed the door. Leaning her back against it, she said aloud, "Betty, you were a fool to ever marry Hale Wilson in the first place! It was stupid, stupid, *stupid!*"

Crossing the room, she sat down in the chair again. Her thoughts ran back over her expectations for her marriage. Hale was undoubtedly the most responsible man she had ever had the opportunity to marry, but life in an army fort had turned out to be much less exciting than she had hoped. She had dreamed of pomp and glory on the frontier as the wife of an army officer. There were supposed to be dinners and dances, with plenty of uniformed men wanting to swing her around the floor. Her dreams had withered in the dismal existence of a lonely outpost, where a woman's greatest excitement was supposed to be attending hen parties and sewing bees with other army wives. Chuckling to herself, she figured she had missed the most exciting thing she could have done as an army wife since coming here: attend Martha Johnston's funeral.

Raised in Los Angeles, Betty was accustomed to city life with its gala occasions, such as banquets, dances, and musical concerts. She was used to prancing down avenues of lavish shops and stores in fancy clothing. With her exquisite beauty, she had found no end of attention from men and had enjoyed the luxury of having her pick of the drooling males who constantly surrounded her.

When Hale Wilson had come along, looking so dashing and gallant in his sharp blue uniform, he had swept Betty off her feet. But as she reflected on her three years of marriage to the tall, muscular army officer, she realized that she had fooled herself on three counts.

For one thing, she had thought she was deeply in love with the handsome captain. Now she realized that she had been in love with the uniform.

Secondly, Betty had told herself that being so in love with Hale, she would not need the attention of other men. But since her feelings for him had lost their luster, she knew she could never be happy without several men dangling on her string.

And finally, Betty had convinced herself that being so in love with the striking captain, she would be happy anywhere with him. But now Fort Bowie seemed like a prison camp in this dry, dismal, dusty, boring desert. *Dry*, she thought with a tight smile. *Well, it has been dry most of the time. Rain is a rare thing in this hellish dust bowl.*

Leaping from her chair, she swore again, picking up a vase that bore a single yellow desert flower. Dashing the vase against the nearest wall, she said aloud, "I hate this awful, ugly place! I hate everything about it! I hate the cacti, the sagebrush, the lizards, the rattlesnakes, and the blazing sun! I hate it! And I hate the man who brought me here!"

Breathing heavily from her outburst of anger, the voluptuous woman reassured herself with one thought: Somehow she was going to get out of this horrible place. She was going to get out of Arizona and go home to Los Angeles. She would divorce Hale Wilson, that miserable, jealous drudge, and she would have herself a fling . . . a *big* one! Then she would find herself a rich man and marry his bank account. From now on, she was going to look out for herself. When she found the right rich man and became his wife, she would bide her time. And then—when things were just right—the sucker would have an accidental death, and she would become a rich widow!

Walking across the room to a full-length mirror, the vivacious blond woman smiled at her reflection. "Yes, ma'am," she said, admiring what she saw, "you are going to find a way out of this miserable prison. You are going to get out of here!"

Chapter Five

Brondo and his five companions ducked their heads and hunched their bodies against the driving rain as they neared the southern tip of the Dragoon Mountains. The Apaches and their horses were completely soaked.

Cochise's third son hardly noticed the rain. His mind was on the beautiful half-breed whose life he had saved. Rayva Johnston was the most beautiful woman he had ever seen, and he kept reliving those moments just after the rescue, when she clung so tightly to him . . . and the smile she gave him when the hotheaded young lieutenant was taking her away. He still carried the warmth of that smile in his heart. One thing he knew for sure: He had to see her again.

Clouds were hanging low, hiding the peaks of the Dragoons and giving their lonely vastness a ghostly appearance. Torrents of water were rumbling down their crevices and low spots in a relentless cascade, making rushing creeks and streams where a few hours before the ground had been cracked and dry.

As the six Apaches rode into the mouth of the canyon that led to the Chiricahua fortress, Brondo eyed the steep slopes rising up on both sides. The heavily shadowed walls, glistening with rain, signified emptiness and a lack of life. But Brondo and his companions knew that Cochise's sentries were there, eyes peeled for any intruders who might attempt to enter their sacred citadel.

Soon the camp came into view, and the mounted Apaches went their separate ways to find rest and dry clothing in their crude adobe shacks. As Brondo drew near his father's lodge, he caught sight of Cochise standing in the doorway. The Chiricahua chief motioned for his son to come to him. Still astride his big Appaloosa, Brondo swung close and reined in.

"Put your horse in the corral," said Cochise in a voice slightly deeper than that of his third son. "We have important business."

Brondo nodded and then guided the magnificent animal toward the corral, where a large number of horses were bunched together with their tails toward the wind. The muscular Apache slid from the Appaloosa's wet back, led it through the gate, and removed the bridle. He hung the bridle on the pole fence, closed the gate, and headed in the rain for his father's lodge.

Cochise's abode, the largest building in the Apache camp, was often used as a gathering place when tribal leaders came for important powwows. From the strange horses tied in front of Cochise's lodge, Brondo knew something significant was taking place.

Lightning flared with an eerie light as Brondo entered the door of the lodge. Thunder followed, shaking the building with its power. By the yellow light of three lanterns, which hung on the walls, Brondo saw that a powwow was in progress. His two older brothers, Nachise and Naiche, were there along with two of the most important warriors of the entire Apache nation. One was Mangas, virile chief of the Mimbres Apaches. The other was Geronimo, the Chiricahuas' most aggressive and bloody warrior. There were also four other Mimbres warriors, sitting silently in a corner.

The black eyes of every man turned to Brondo as he came through the door. The important ones were seated in the center of the floor in a semicircle, and Cochise was still on his feet. He set his dark, marblelike eyes on his third son and said, "Where have you been?"

Brondo pulled his gaze from the others to his stalwart father. Cochise was forty-nine years old but still had the mien and strength of a man half his age. He stood an even six feet in height, as did Brondo, while the other two sons were some two inches shorter. Whenever Brondo looked at his father, a touch of awe was present in his heart along with a sense of deep admiration. There was something commanding about the dark-skinned Chiricahua chief's appearance. Cochise was a born leader and a man of great courage and determination; his piercing black eyes, the square cut of his jaw, and the way he carried himself were all manifestations of these traits.

In answer to his father's question Brondo replied, "My companions and I have been observing a funeral and burial at Fort Bowie's cemetery."

A wry smile curved Cochise's lips. "Good!" he exclaimed. "Another bluecoat is dead?"

Shaking his head slowly, Brondo said, "It was not a bluecoat, my father."

"No?" Cochise's smile drained away.

"There was no bugle to play—what do they call it?"

"Taps," spoke up the swarthy Geronimo from his place on the floor.

Nodding, Brondo said to his father, "There were no taps played and no twenty-one gun salute. This would tell me that the burial was of a civilian rather than a bluecoat."

Cochise batted his eyes slowly in agreement and said, "Brondo should dry himself off and then join us. We are in an important discussion."

Brondo was well acquainted with his father's abode and knew where to find cloth to dry himself. Wheeling, he disappeared into a small adjoining room. There in the dark shadows stood his mother, Arizpenora, already holding out a cloth for his use. Smiling warmly at her, he accepted it and began wiping rainwater from his hair and face, dabbing at his buckskin shirt and pants. He smiled again at his mother as he handed her the cloth. In return she reached up and stroked his cheek. He squeezed her hand, adjusted his headband, and returned to the large room.

Brondo had purposely refrained from telling his father about saving the life of Colonel Brett Johnston's daughter.

Cochise harbored a bitter hatred toward the colonel, and his wrath would be stirred toward his third son if he learned of the incident. White people were to be killed, not spared.

Cochise was still standing when Brondo entered the large room. The lantern light caused the chief's awesome shadow to float on the buff-colored adobe wall behind him. Gesturing for Brondo to take a spot on the floor next to where he would sit, Cochise waited until his son was in place and then eased down into a cross-legged position.

While the others listened Cochise said, "Brondo, we have been discussing the white ranchers coming into our territory one by one. Geronimo has counted fifteen new ranches between the southern tip of the Dragoon Mountains and the town of Tombstone. They are too close to us."

Brondo's shoulders sagged. He knew what his father was about to say.

"The ranchers must be killed!" Cochise said with furor. "If they are allowed to live, more whites will move into the territory!" Pointing across the circle, he grunted, "Mangas and his Mimbres warriors are going to help the Chiricahuas. Bands of Apaches will hit all fifteen ranches at exactly the same time."

Brondo knew that several bands of Chiricahuas were out scouting, raiding wagon trains and killing mail carriers; hence, his father had sought help from the Mimbres to strike fast and hard at the ranchers.

Cochise's dark face was a mask of animosity. Showing his teeth, he spoke harshly, "The ranchers and their families are to be massacred! Their buildings are to be burned! No one is to be spared! We will wipe them out, and then we will fortify ourselves for the retaliation that will come from the army."

As his father spoke, Brondo's gaze strayed to the faces of Nachise and Naiche. A wicked gleam filled their eyes, and Brondo knew that like their father they were eager to shed the blood of white men. He was keenly aware of the vast difference between himself and his half brothers: They were savage and heartless like Cochise, while Brondo, who had proven himself a brave and fearless warrior when battling soldiers, found it difficult to attack and kill civilians . . . especially women and children.

Brondo attributed the difference between himself and his two brothers to their different mothers. Nahlekadeya, Cochise's first wife, had borne him Nachise and Naiche. She had died when the two boys were quite young, and Cochise had then married Arizpenora, who had borne him two daughters and then Brondo.

Nahlekadeya had been high spirited and short of temper, and her two sons had inherited these traits. In this respect Brondo was like his mother, Arizpenora, who was docile and quiet. But while Nachise and Naiche physically resembled their mother, Brondo was the spitting image of Cochise.

Excited about the raid, Cochise said to Geronimo, "Let us see the map you and your scouts have drawn up."

Brondo watched as the grim-faced warrior rose to his knees and produced a rolled piece of paper. Geronimo, who had a killer instinct and a powerful, riveting personality, was keen to slaughter the ranchers, and his hand shook as he rolled out the broad sheet of paper. Brondo could see the location of the fifteen ranches on Geronimo's crude map, each identified by an X. They were scattered south of the Dragoons, which were indicated by a series of tentlike marks.

As Mangas, Nachise, Naiche, and Brondo leaned forward to get a clear view of the map, Cochise rose to his knees to peer over it and lay out the plan of attack. Mangas and his Mimbres would attack nine of the ranches— those to the south—while each of the six Chiricahuas present would lead a band against a ranch to the north. Pointing to one X at a time, Cochise showed them the ranch he and his band would wipe out, and then assigned ranches to Nachise, Naiche, and Geronimo.

Cochise knew that his third son had an aversion to killing nonmilitary men and women and children, but ignoring the aversion, he pointed to the last X and said emphatically, "And this ranch, Brondo, will be yours to exterminate."

Nachise and Naiche furtively glanced at Brondo and then turned back to the map.

"We will attack the fifteen ranches at the same moment," said Cochise. "At high sun tomorrow."

Brondo felt a cold ball form in his stomach but did not allow it to register on his face. Feeling the eyes of the others upon him, he studied the map.

"Any questions?" asked Cochise.

No one spoke.

"All right," said the Chiricahua chief. "We each have a task to accomplish. If we do our jobs well, no more whites will settle on our land. We will meet back here tomorrow when the sun is midway in the afternoon sky. At that time we will prepare ourselves for the onslaught that will come from Colonel Johnston and his bluecoats by the next day."

One by one the Indians rose and filed out, but Brondo lingered behind. When the others had gone, Cochise gestured toward his son and asked, "Did you want to speak to me, Brondo?"

As always Brondo found himself in awe of the venerable chief's presence. "Yes, my father," he replied. "There is something I must discuss with you."

While Brondo paused, searching for the exact words to use, Cochise studied him with perceptive eyes, and a warm flush of pride and pleasure washed over him. Brondo was tall and sinewy, with the same broad chest and muscular frame as his sire. Their facial features were strikingly similar, both having the same high cheekbones and an aquiline nose. Nachise and Naiche were rugged men of whom Cochise was proud, but their features were more rounded, and their faces tended to be oval rather than angular. Nachise, who by birthright would be the next chief of the Chiricahuas, was by far more fierce in nature than Brondo, as was Naiche. But there was not a warrior among the Apache nation who was as strong or adept at hand-to-hand combat as the youthful Brondo.

Cochise had often found himself wishing that Brondo had been his firstborn. There was about him an air of dignity and grace that was lacking in Nachise, and physically Brondo was the more attractive of the two. As far as Cochise could see, Brondo's only flaw was the lack of killer instinct. He already knew what his handsome son was going to say.

"It is not the desire of your youngest son to disobey your orders, but it is against his sense of fairness to murder ranchers and their families."

Keeping his poise, Cochise said in a level tone, "There is no choice in this matter, my son. If we do not annihilate the ranchers, more will come. Soon we will be forced from the land that has been ours for two hundred years."

"I do not like the white infiltration any more than you do, my father," said Brondo. "But I must tell you that to kill the fifteen ranchers and their wives and children will accomplish nothing. More whites will come to replace them."

Cochise squinted his eyes, not liking what he was hearing. Curtly he snapped, "I do not like your words!"

"My father," said the young warrior, "in the white man's sacred book there is a story of a wicked chief who defied the Great Spirit. One night during a time of carousal and gaiety, the hand of the Great Spirit came into the chief's dwelling and wrote on the wall a message of doom. The wicked chief died violently that night. From that story, white men have developed a saying. When something is quite obviously going to take place, they say that *the handwriting is on the wall.*"

The Chiricahua chief mumbled, "Maybe I have made a mistake allowing you to learn how to read white men's words. You wanted to educate yourself about our enemy, and that is admirable, but perhaps this has gone too far." Rubbing his chin and eyeing his son speculatively, he asked, "What are you trying to say with this story of the handwriting on the wall?"

"My father," Brondo answered, "for the Apache the handwriting is on the wall. Our liberty to roam this great land freely without intrusion by the whites is rapidly coming to an end."

Cochise bristled, baring his teeth. An animallike growl

escaped his lips. "Brondo speaks with foolish tongue! There is no handwriting on the wall! The Apache nation and our Indian allies will drive the pale-faced intruders back to where they came from!"

Shaking his head, Brondo said, "My father, we have discussed this before. You know we have, many times. Your youngest son means no disrespect, but you must open your eyes and face the facts. The white man's invasion of our land increases from moon to moon. If we kill ten, a hundred come in their place. If we continue to take up our weapons against them, they will one day overwhelm us in number and annihilate us. If we try to fight the whites, we will be like grass that has been burned at the roots. The wind will blow us away until there are no Apaches left."

Anger purpled Cochise's face as he rasped, "Is Brondo, son of Cochise, suggesting that the Apache lie down and die? That we tuck our tails like whipped cur dogs and not fight for what is ours?"

Wiping a nervous hand over his mouth, Brondo shook his head. "No, my father, this is not what I am suggesting. I do not want to see our people driven from the land and destroyed. What I propose is not cowardly surrender but intelligent negotiation. It must be done before it is too late and the Apache become a lost people in the history books of the white man."

The hot eyes of Cochise held steady on his son.

Continuing an attempt to reason with his father, Brondo said, "By massacring the ranchers, we will only bring white soldiers in greater strength and numbers against us. The whites seem to have unlimited resources of men, horses, weapons, and ammunition—and we do not."

The chief's rage hit the boiling point. Lashing at Brondo with words that cracked like a bullwhip, he blared, "Has Brondo forgotten what the bluecoats did to his uncle Naretena and his cousins Mogollo and Hildago eleven grasses ago? They were innocent of any crime against the whites, but they were hanged!"

Brondo could only blink his eyes. No words would check Cochise's flow of angry words.

"You know what our ancestors have taught us about hanging, Brondo," continued the furious chief. "When a man dies by hanging, his spirit is choked up inside the body and trapped there. The spirit dies and rots inside the body and cannot fly away freely to the land of the sky. White-eyes Lieutenant George Bascom did this to your uncle and his sons!" Swinging an angry fist, Cochise railed hotly, "I will never forgive the whites for what they did! Never! I will fight them until the last breath leaves my body!"

Brondo caught a glimpse of his mother peeking around the door frame of the small room where she had waited out the conference. He recognized fear in her eyes as she listened to her husband's fury.

Cochise turned his back on Brondo and stood with his palms against the wall, breathing hard. With bitterness clinging to his heart like a leech, he let his thoughts roll back to January of 1861. . . .

A band of Pinal Apaches had ridden onto a ranch just across the San Pedro River to the west and had stolen several head of cattle. They had also kidnapped a ten-year-old boy named Felix, the son of the rancher's Mexican mistress. The rancher, whose name was John Ward, somehow had the mistaken notion that the kidnappers were Cochise and his Chiricahuas, and he reported the incident that way at nearby Fort Buchanan. The commandant there hated Cochise and readily accepted Ward's word that Cochise and his men were the thieves and kidnappers.

Shortly thereafter, a young lieutenant named George Bascom was sent from Fort Buchanan with fifty-four men to find the kidnappers. Along with Ward they headed for Apache Pass, a passage just south of Fort Bowie between the Dragoon and Chiricahua mountains with an elevation of about fifty-one hundred feet. Bascom, eager to make a name for himself, vowed he would get back the Mexican boy and Ward's cattle if he had to tear the mountains apart to find them.

Arriving at Apache Pass, Lieutenant Bascom halted his column at the Butterfield stagecoach station there. He told a stage driver who was acquainted with Cochise that he and his men were on a routine patrol, heading toward the Rio Grande. They would be camping in a nearby canyon and would welcome a visit from the Chiricahua chief.

Cochise's scouts had quickly reported the large number of soldiers in the area, and before long Cochise himself was at the station, asking what the soldiers were doing there. The stagecoach driver assured Cochise that he had nothing to fear from the lieutenant and passed on Bascom's words that he would welcome a visit from Cochise.

The Chiricahua chief decided to take the lieutenant up on his invitation. He set out for where the soldiers were camped, accompanied by his wife, Nahlekadeya; his brother Naretena; his seventeen-year-old son, Nachise; and Naretena's two young sons, Mogollo and Hildago.

Making their way among the yuccas and granite boulders, the Apaches entered the canyon where the soldiers were bivouacked. Four men in blue stepped out in front of them as they came upon the camp, but before the soldiers could speak, Cochise raised his hand in a sign of peace and said, "I am Cochise of the Chiricahuas." Swinging his hand in a sweeping motion toward his companions, he added, "This is my wife, Nahlekadeya, and my son, Nachise. This is my brother Naretena, and his sons, Mogollo and Hildago. We come by invitation of your lieutenant."

"Just a minute," spoke one of the soldiers. Cochise waited while he ran to a large tent and disappeared inside. Seconds later he returned and in a friendly manner bid the Indians to dismount and enter Bascom's tent.

The lieutenant was on his feet when Cochise and the others came through the opening. He smiled amiably and said, "Please, sit down."

Cochise sat down on the earthen floor, expecting to have polite conversation with the young lieutenant. As everyone sat cross-legged the chief introduced himself and his companions to Bascom. John Ward, who had remained in the background, chose this moment to slip out of the tent and tell Bascom's men to surround it.

The inexperienced lieutenant sat facing Cochise, and without preliminary conversation he scowled and said, "I know you and your men stole the cattle of rancher John Ward. You also kidnapped the son of a Mexican woman who lives on the ranch. I demand that you return the boy and the animals at once."

Cochise's head snapped up. He was astounded at the accusation. "What cattle? What boy? I know nothing of what the lieutenant speaks."

Angered by what he thought was Indian deceit, the headstrong Bascom repeated his charge. Again Cochise denied any knowledge of the cattle or the boy, calmly assuring the lieutenant that he would ask other Apaches about the incident and try to free the boy and return the cattle.

Bascom's eyes narrowed and filled with contempt. "Cochise, you're a dirty liar!" he boomed. "Until the boy and the cattle are returned, you and the others here are our prisoners!"

Cochise's features turned to stone, his black eyes cold and ominous. "Cochise does not lie!" he bellowed. "You have no right to hold us prisoner!"

"My word stands," said Bascom doggedly.

Cochise knew he could accomplish nothing as Bascom's prisoner. Infuriated, he drew a knife from his moccasin legging, slashed through the tent wall, and scrambled outside. Dashing past the stunned soldiers, he mounted his horse and vanished into the canyon. His family, who were unable to follow him, remained as Bascom's prisoners.

As the furious chief rode hard for the Chiricahua fortress in the Dragoons, he plotted how to take revenge on the stagecoach driver at Apache Pass—the man he held responsible for luring him and his family into Bascom's trap. After gathering a band of his men at the stronghold, he led them to the stage station at Apache Pass and called for those inside to come out. The driver, Jim Wallace, was smiling as he walked out the door; he was totally unaware of what had happened at Bascom's tent and had no reason to fear Cochise. With him were two other men, Charles Culver and Ben Walsh.

Wallace's smile faded when he saw the look on Cochise's face. Culver and Walsh broke for the station, but the Apache opened fire and cut them down. Wallace's face blanched white and sweat beaded his brow as he gasped, "Cochise . . . what is wrong?"

Two Apaches laid strong hands on Wallace, disarming him. Cochise stepped close and said through clenched teeth, "You betrayed me, Wallace!"

"N-no!" stammered the stage driver. "I did no such thing, Cochise!"

"White-eyes liar!" fumed the angry chief. "With your help, the scheming lieutenant lured us into his camp and took us prisoner. He accused me of stealing some rancher's cattle and a boy. Lies! I broke free, but the soldiers still hold my family."

"C-Cochise, I did not know Bascom was going to do this!" insisted Wallace. "You must believe me!"

Regarding him coldly, the chief snarled, "White men were born with forked tongues! You lie!"

Determined to win the freedom of his family, Cochise had his men put Wallace on a horse and ride toward the canyon. Soon they came upon eight Mexicans and two white men in a small wagon train, which the Apaches quickly surrounded. Cochise took the two white men as prisoners. Under his sharp command, his warriors tied the eight Mexicans to the wheels of their wagons and torched their clothing, leaving them to burn to death. As they rode on toward the canyon, they could hear the Mexicans screaming as flames enveloped them.

Halting just outside the camp, Cochise tied a lariat around Jim Wallace's neck and led him to where the soldiers could see the two of them. Shouting at the top of his voice, Cochise said to the group of soldiers who gathered at the edge of the camp, "Tell your lieutenant I want to talk to him!"

Bascom was summoned, and when he stood among his soldiers, Cochise shouted, "I have your friend Wallace! I also have two other white men as prisoners! You will release my family immediately, or these men will die!"

Bascom, totally inexperienced in handling Indians, shouted back, "No deal, savage! When you bring the boy and the cattle, you get your family! And not until!"

In a frenzy, Jim Wallace shouted, "Bascom! Don't do this! He'll kill me! Please! Let Cochise's family go!"

Ignoring the stage driver's desperate plea, Bascom pointed a stiff finger at the swarthy chief and said, "You're a liar, Cochise. If you don't produce that Mexican boy and those cattle today, your wife and son and the others will be executed!" With that, the brash young lieutenant wheeled and disappeared into his tent.

Cochise realized that negotiation with Lieutenant George Bascom was futile. While Wallace pleaded for mercy the Apaches dragged him and the other two white men into a rock-strewn enclosure. Then, taking a feather-adorned war lance from the hand of one of his men, Cochise eyed the white men with hatred. The sun shone on the lance's sharp silver tip, glistening like eyes of vengeance. Gritting his teeth and growling, Cochise ran all three of them through several times.

Leaving the bodies to rot in the sun, Cochise and his Chiricahuas rode away.

An hour later Bascom sent some of his men to see if they could find any sign of what had happened in the rock enclosure. From the camp they had heard the death screams of the three white men. When the soldiers returned with the three mutilated bodies, the young lieutenant went into a rage and promptly ordered Naretena, Mogollo, and Hildago hanged.

While the three Apaches were being strung up, Bascom spoke to Nahlekadeya, saying, "I am going to let you and your son go free. You tell Cochise that I hanged his brother and nephews in retaliation for the three white men he massacred. I am sparing the two of you so that your husband will see that we whites are not as brutal as you Apaches. Tell your husband to think it over before he starts a full-scale war over this incident."

Nahlekadeya and Nachise stood in silence and watched

the soldiers mount up and ride out of Apache Pass. When
the cloud of dust settled, they mounted their horses and
headed for home.

Cochise and his small band had returned to the Chiricahua camp and gathered a hundred warriors. He had
decided to storm the army camp and free his family by
slaughtering all of the soldiers. They did not see Nahlekadeya and Nachise before they rode out.

When the Apaches arrived at the spot where the army
had camped, they found that the soldiers were gone.
Naretena, Mogollo, and Hildago were hanging from the
limb of a huge oak tree. Cochise's wrath was enflamed.

Thus began the Apache war against white men. Cochise
embarked on a bloody campaign to drive the hated whites
from his land forever. Within two months of the hangings
Cochise and his Chiricahuas had killed one hundred and
fifty whites, attacking stagecoaches, wagon trains, mines,
ranches, and small settlements. The southeastern Arizona
desert was washed with the blood of white men, women,
and children.

In the years that followed, many soldiers, mail riders,
prospectors, immigrants, and stagecoach crews and passengers died violently at the hands of the vindictive Apaches.
Stagecoach drivers and shotgunners were offered triple
pay to command the route through Apache Pass, and
many of them never lived to collect it. During these same
years, many bloody confrontations took place between the
soldiers at Fort Bowie and the Chiricahua warriors, and a
bitter rivalry and hatred grew between Colonel Brett Johnston and Cochise.

Cochise let his thoughts come back to the present. He
turned around to see Brondo still standing behind him.
The roar of the rain on the roof had become a soft patter-
ing. Speaking in a monotone to his third son, the dark-
eyed chief said, "Brondo, it has been eleven grasses since
the soldiers hanged your uncle and cousins. I have fought
the fork-tongued whites all this time. We cannot trust

them. I tried negotiating with them once. I will never do it again. The Chiricahuas will fight to the death."

"But my father," pleaded Brondo, "they will come with great numbers and—"

"Enough!" spat Cochise, holding palms up to his son. "The fifteen ranches will be attacked at midday tomorrow. And you will wipe out the ranchers that I have appointed to you!"

Chapter Six

The rain was letting up as Captain Hale Wilson and Lieutenant Clifford Murdock stood at attention in the office of Colonel Brett Johnston. The two officers were still caked with mud, blood, and horse manure following their fight behind the stable.

Showing frustration and some temper, the colonel said, "You two stink to high heaven! I ought to confine you to the brig for six months for this. Fine examples you are as officers of the United States Army! I have a hard enough time keeping the enlisted men from using each other as punching bags. Now you drop a new hot potato in my lap!"

The two filthy officers remained rigidly at attention, both avoiding the colonel's burning glare. They kept their line of sight behind him, at a spot where the wall joined the ceiling.

"And if you had to fight," fumed Johnston, "why in the name of common sense did you have to do it in the corral? Especially while it was raining?"

Neither man ventured an answer.

The colonel cleared his throat. "Now I want to know what this fight was about."

Hale Wilson did not want to involve Betty, and since he had punished Murdock to his own satisfaction, he was not willing to cause him further trouble. Still holding his eyes

61

aloft, he said, "We had a personal difference, sir. It is settled now."

Pressing authority into his voice, the colonel snapped, "Maybe you have some of those horse droppings in your ears, Captain! Didn't you hear what I said? I said I want to know what this fight was about!"

"It was personal, sir," repeated the captain. "I would rather just leave it at that."

Johnston sighed, running his fingers through his silver hair. "I am going to ask you a question, Captain Wilson," he said stiffly. "And I want a straight, honest answer."

Hale swallowed hard. "Yes, sir."

Narrowing his eyes and pulling his lips into a thin line, Fort Bowie's commandant asked, "Is Mrs. Wilson involved in this dispute?"

Hale Wilson was having a hard time finding his voice. He hated what was going on behind his back in his home.

Murdock spoke up. "This thing is my fault, Colonel. I have had occasion to visit Mrs. Wilson in her quarters when the captain is absent. I have just been severely punished by the captain for so doing. And rightly so, I might add. He had every right to give me a good whipping, and he did just that. I will not be seeing Mrs. Wilson alone again."

Johnston stared at the lieutenant for a long moment. Murdock still held his gaze toward the wall behind the colonel. Johnston barked, "Look at me, Murdock!"

The lieutenant dropped his line of sight until it leveled with the blazing eyes of his commanding officer. Curling a lip over his teeth, Johnston said with gravel in his voice, "You stink in more than one way, Lieutenant Murdock! Get out of my sight. You are dismissed."

Clifford Murdock saluted, wheeled, and hastened out the door.

The colonel turned his attention to Hale Wilson, who remained at attention. He looked him up and down and then turned away to avoid the stench that was coming from his muck-covered body. With his back to him, the colonel said, "Hale, what is the problem between you and Betty? Why is she continuously carrying on with other men?"

"Well, sir," Hale said cautiously, "Betty . . . Betty—"

"You don't have to stand at attention anymore, Hale," cut in Johnston. "Just relax and answer my question."

The captain's head bobbed. He released a faint smile and said, "Sir, it's Betty's background. Her flirtations with the men on the post are a result of the way she was before I married her. She was somewhat wild . . . and fancy-free. She's just having a little trouble adjusting to married life. She'll be all right in time."

"Don't put up a smoke screen with me, son," said the silver-haired commandant. "Betty will not be all right in time unless you do something in a positive way to correct the situation. I want to help you, and I have a suggestion."

"Thank you, Colonel," Hale said smiling weakly. "I'm open to anything."

"You need to encourage Betty to spend time with the women of the fort. She keeps herself absolutely aloof from them. If she would make friends with them and do things that women do, she would be less interested in the men. Of course, with Martha gone there are only three other women. But I'm sure Rayva and the other two would welcome Betty's companionship."

"You're right, sir," agreed Hale. "I'll begin encouraging her right away along these lines."

Johnston turned around and smiled broadly. "The women are going into Bowie tomorrow for a sewing bee with the women of the town. I'm sure Mrs. Benedict, Mrs. Simmons, and Rayva would love to have her accompany them. They will be escorted to Bowie by a squad of troopers under Sergeant Clyde Steadman."

Nodding, Hale said, "Sounds good, sir. I'll tell Betty about it and encourage her to go. Thank you for your concern." As he spoke he offered his hand, but the colonel looked down at the slime-wet hand and flared his nostrils. "Oh, I . . . I'm sorry, sir." Hale grinned sheepishly, withdrawing the hand.

The colonel cleared his throat and said, "If I were you, I would take a dip in the water trough at the corral before I went home, Hale."

Grinning again, the captain backed out the door with a weak salute.

"Sewing bee!" blustered Betty, her eyes flashing fire. "Where do you get the unmitigated gall to tell me I ought to go to a stupid hen party?"

"Now calm down, Betty," Hale said. He was still wearing his wet clothing. "I just—"

The irate blonde swore vehemently, kicked over a small end table, and turned to face him. "I am not going, Hale! Do you hear me? I am not going!"

"Will you listen to me a minute?" Hale lashed back. "I'm just trying to put some variety in your life."

Betty, angry beyond words, pivoted, marched to the bedroom, and slammed the door violently.

Hale remembered that he needed to check on some things at the supply shack. He wanted first to get into some clean clothes, but he was not in the frame of mind to face the wrath of the wildcat who lurked behind the bedroom door. Tapping on the door, he called, "Betty, I'm going over to the supply shack. I'll be back in about half an hour." There was no response. "Betty!" he repeated.

"Okay! Okay!" came her sharp reply. "I hear you! Go on!"

Shaking his head, the flustered husband turned and left.

Across the compound, furtive eyes watched the captain's quarters from an office at the fort headquarters. It was Lieutenant Donald Simmons, husband of one of the three remaining women at the fort. His office was directly beside the commandant's, which had enabled him to hear through the thin walls the entire conversation between Colonel Johnston and the two officers.

The rain had ended when Hale Wilson came outside and started toward the supply shack. As soon as he turned the corner and was swallowed by the night, Lieutenant Simmons slipped along the edge of the shadows and tapped on the door of the Wilson quarters. When he got no response, he knocked louder. Presently he heard light footsteps coming toward the door. The latch rattled, and Betty's beautiful face appeared as the door came open.

"Oh, Don! It's you!" she exclaimed. "Come in."

Simmons looked around to see if anyone was nearby and then quickly stepped inside and shut the door. Betty threw her arms around him, saying, "Darling, I'm so glad to see you!"

As she presented her lips for a kiss, Simmons jerked her arms from around his neck and shoved her away. A sullen anger was evident in his eyes. A prominent vein was standing out on his forehead, and thick color reddened his neck.

Betty gasped in surprise, batting her well-painted eyes. "Don, darling, what's the matter?"

"Betty," he said, a whisper of rage coming into his voice, "I found out today that you've been seeing Cliff Murdock."

The blond woman stiffened. Looking totally shocked, she said, "Darling, I don't know what you're talking about. There's been some kind of a misunderstanding somewhere."

"There sure has," he said coldly. "I misunderstood your feelings about me!"

"Don," she gasped, "I haven't been—"

"Don't lie to me, Betty!" he breathed hotly. "I heard the whole thing today through the wall of the colonel's office. Your husband beat up real bad on Murdock. Both of them were called on the carpet for fighting." He paused and then gripped her by the shoulders. "I thought you were in love with me."

Betty Wilson did not want to lose her hold on Don Simmons. In his position as cashier of the army quartermaster corps, he was close to the army's money, since he was responsible for the payroll for each of the thirteen forts in Arizona Territory. And anyone who even worked close to money attracted her. Moving close to him and speaking softly, she said, "Let me explain something to you, darling. I *am* in love with you—only you—but until you can get rid of your wife so we can have each other, I don't dare let Hale find out about us. See, he knows about my little flirtations with other men, and by keeping his attention on those meaningless little escapades, I can cover *our* relationship."

Betty looked up innocently at Simmons with her deep-blue eyes, reading his expression to see if her carefully chosen words had taken effect. He was still giving her a harsh look.

Moving even closer, she laid a hand on his shoulder and lovingly stroked his face with the fingertips of her other hand. Lowering her eyelids, she said, "I really do love you with all of my heart, Don. You're the only man I've ever really loved. I thought I was in love with Hale until you came along. Don't you understand? What I do is for you and me. Cliff Murdock means nothing to me. It's you, my darling. Only you."

The unscrupulous woman watched the fire leave Don Simmons's eyes. His face muscles relaxed under her touch, and the stiffness in his body began to slacken. Knowing she had melted him, she ran a fingertip over the outline of his mouth and said, "Now . . . kiss me and tell me everything is all right."

Blinded by Betty's beauty and cunning, Lieutenant Donald Simmons succumbed to her deception. Roughly taking hold of her, he kissed her passionately. When their lips parted, he breathed, "Oh, Betty, I'm crazy about you!"

"That's better." She smiled. "I'm crazy about you, too, my darling." She paused a moment as he held her, and then she asked, "Don?"

"Yes?"

"Has your wife guessed that there is someone else?"

"Naw," he chuckled. "Elizabeth is easy to fool. She has no idea."

"You must still be showing her a lot of affection," Betty said, pushing her lips into a pout.

"I have to," he responded, "or she'll suspect. I'll just be glad when you and I can be together without having to sneak around."

"That day will come, my darling," she cooed. "We must be patient."

Simmons kissed her again and then asked, "How soon will Hale be back?"

"In another twenty minutes or so."

"Then I must tell you quickly that I'll be leaving on a trip to California in two days."

"Oh?"

"I'll be taking the Butterfield stage to Los Angeles, carrying a one hundred thousand dollar payroll."

Betty did a swift intake of breath. "A hundred thousand?"

"Yes. The money is going to an army installation near San Bernardino. I'll be gone about three weeks."

Betty had started to comment when suddenly they heard heavy footsteps approaching the door. "Hale!" she whispered. "He's back early!"

Before Simmons could react, the door swung open. The captain's eyes widened momentarily, and then his face turned to granite. Fixing the lieutenant with augerlike eyes, he drew his lips hard against his teeth and growled, "What are you doing here?"

Before the guilty man could speak, Betty leaped between them, saying quickly, "Lieutenant Simmons has come to see you, darling. I was just telling him he could find you at the supply shack." Betty hoped Simmons could think fast enough to convince Hale she was telling the truth.

The lieutenant's mind was working furiously. As smoothly as possible, Simmons said, "As you know, sir, I am putting in an order for some horses for the fort. I was just wondering if everything is all right with your horse, or would you like for me to have one included special for you in the bunch?"

Eyeing him suspiciously, Hale Wilson said, "This couldn't have waited until tomorrow, Lieutenant? I mean, I am in and out of the colonel's office a dozen times a day. I pass right by your door each time. You couldn't have stopped me one of those times and asked about this?"

"Well, Captain," Simmons said, holding his voice steady, "I'm working on the papers tonight, trying to get them ready. I need to carry them on the stagecoach with me when I head for California."

"That's two days away," Hale said.

"Well, I know, sir, but I have many other things to tend to before I go, so I was trying to wrap up this order as quickly as possible."

Hale stared at him wordlessly.

"Look, Captain," Simmons said, smiling weakly, "if there is something I've done wrong, I—"

"Forget it," butted in Hale. "I'm perfectly satisfied with my horse. You won't need to order one for me."

"All right, sir," said Simmons, backing through the door. "Thank you."

As her husband stared after the lieutenant, Betty Wilson could see in his eyes that he was not convinced. He was still suspicious, she realized, but without proof probably figured there was nothing he could do. When he shut the door, she sought to dodge his anger by saying, "Darling, I've decided that you're right about the sewing bee in Bowie. I'm going to go!"

As she spoke, the captivating woman moved into her husband's arms, forcing herself tight up against him. Wrapping her arms around his neck, she said, "Doesn't that make my lover happy?"

The captain felt his defenses crumble. Betty's mysterious power was overcoming him again, and he was so helplessly in love with her that he could not keep a level head in her presence. Shoving aside his doubts, he succumbed to her beauty, and almost crushing her with his powerful arms, he kissed her with fire and passion.

The sun was lifting the top of its fiery rim over the eastern horizon, staining the scattered clouds a brilliant orange as Brondo rode alone out of the Dragoon Mountains, headed in the direction of Fort Bowie. He had to see Rayva Johnston again. He had lain awake most of the night reliving the few moments he had held her in his arms at the cliff's edge. The sweetness of the smile she had given him while riding away remained warm in his memory.

The drops of moisture in the trees picked up the early morning sunlight and glistened like diamonds. The air was pungent and clean from the washing the rain had given it the day before. Tiny rivulets were still trickling along the cracks in the ground.

Brondo loved the Arizona desert. There was a wildness to it that spoke to a kindred spirit within him. He had never known any feeling to surpass his kinship with the rugged and beautiful land until the dark-eyed daughter of Colonel Brett Johnston had unwittingly plucked a string in his heart.

His thoughts on Rayva, Brondo wondered again why an army colonel would have been married to an Indian. He reckoned from what he had seen of Rayva's features that her mother had been an Apache.

Riding along on his huge Appaloosa, Brondo thought again of saving Rayva's life and of the warmth of her lovely body as he held her close, until she slid to the ground to ride away with the insolent young lieutenant. In his mind, he saw again the colonel's friendly smile, which had evaporated when he heard that Brondo was a son of Cochise.

Brondo thought of the many battles in which he had fought where Colonel Brett Johnston was present. He figured that, to Johnston, all Indians probably looked alike. The colonel most likely did not remember having seen Brondo amid gunfire, smoke, and dust; even if he had remembered, Brondo's daring act of saving Rayva no doubt would have eased any hard feelings toward him. But it was different when Johnston heard the name of Cochise. Brondo knew the unholy hatred that burned like volcanic fire between his father and Fort Bowie's commandant.

Brondo's only hope was what the colonel had said after Rayva was rescued: *I consider you a friend.* The young Apache hoped that his deed of risking his life to save Rayva would cause Johnston to overlook his relation to Cochise.

The sun had detached itself from the earth's edge and was starting its upward arc when Brondo approached the gate of Fort Bowie. He held his rifle in a vertical position, exposing the white cloth tied near the muzzle.

A blue-uniformed guard appeared on a platform at the top of the stockade fence next to the gate. Eyeing the Apache warily in spite of the white flag, the trooper asked, "Who are you, and what is your business?"

"My name is Brondo," he replied in a friendly manner.

"I am of the Chiricahuas. I have come to ask Colonel Johnston if I may pay a visit to his daughter."

Another guard appeared beside the trooper as he said coldly, "Miss Rayva does not receive Apaches as guests."

"If she knows I am here, she will see me," Brondo argued.

The two men in blue looked at each other, shaking their heads.

Speaking a bit louder, Brondo said, "I am the man who saved her life yesterday. I have only come to see if she is all right after her very trying ordeal."

"She is just fine," said the second trooper. "Now be on your way."

"I have come in peace and earnest concern for the colonel's daughter, white soldier," Brondo said softly. "The colonel told me yesterday that he considers me a friend. If you turn away the colonel's friend, he may be displeased."

"Sure talks fancy for a heathen, don't he?" the second trooper said to the first one.

"Maybe I'd better take him to the colonel," the first one replied.

Seconds later the guard opened the gate and motioned for Brondo to enter. Clucking to the Appaloosa, Brondo moved through the gate.

"Stay astride your horse and follow me," said the trooper.

In less than a minute the guard stopped in front of the colonel's quarters. Soldiers in the compound took note of Brondo and the big black-and-white horse. A buzz was set up among them as they realized this was the man who had saved the colonel's daughter from a horrible death.

The guard looked up at Brondo and said, "You will remain on your horse unless Colonel Johnston tells you to dismount."

Brondo nodded and then watched as the guard stepped up to the door and knocked. Seconds later the tall commandant opened the door, his eyes immediately flicking past the man in blue to the Apache who sat astride the Appaloosa. Johnston's leathery face stiffened.

Throwing a thumb over his shoulder, the guard said,

"The Apache told me that you are friends, sir. I thought it best to—"

"It's all right, Akins," said Johnston. "You may return to your post."

As Trooper Akins skittered away, the silver-haired colonel stepped to the edge of the wooden porch and asked, "Why have you come here, Brondo?" His eyes were like ice.

Looking down at Johnston, Brondo said with a smile, "I am concerned with your daughter's welfare, Colonel. She had a very close call yesterday. Is she all right?"

Eyeing the Apache grimly, Johnston nodded and said, "Rayva is just fine."

Leaning forward a bit, Brondo said, "May I see her, sir?"

The colonel's cheeks tinted, and he said stiffly, "It is not necessary for you to see her."

As the words were still lingering in the warm morning air, Rayva suddenly appeared in the doorway. A broad smile came to her lovely mouth. Gliding rapidly into the sunlight, she touched her father's arm and said, "Father, this brave man saved my life. If it were not for him, you would be burying me today. Of course it is all right if he sees me!"

Colonel Brett Johnston of the United States Army, valiant veteran of many bloody battles, was struck dumb by the petite female. Nonplussed, he watched her step off the porch and move close to the Appaloosa. Smiling up warmly at the handsome young Apache, she said, "I heard Father call you Brondo."

Brondo nodded, already feeling the spell of Rayva's beauty.

"Please get down, Brondo, and come in," she said. "Do you like coffee?"

Chapter Seven

At the Apache camp in the Dragoon Mountains, the women and children looked on with excitement as Cochise's warriors prepared themselves for the attack on the unsuspecting ranchers. Mangas and thirty of his Mimbres were among them. Some were cleaning and loading their weapons, some putting on war paint, and others tending to their horses.

In his adobe hut Geronimo was striping his body with war paint in front of an old cracked mirror he had taken from a wagon train in a raid. While he was running a paint stripe across his nose from cheek to cheek, he could hear a conversation going on near his door. Brondo's five companions, Ramino, Clumin, Eskamin, Bisilo, and Zenta, were discussing Brondo's early morning ride to Fort Bowie.

"His father will be angry," said Zenta. "I wish Brondo had not gone."

"There will be no problem," put in Ramino, "as long as he is back here in time to ride out for the attack on the ranch."

"He will be back in time," said Bisilo with a note of assurance in his voice. Eyeing the position of the sun in the morning sky, he said it again. "He will be back in time."

At that moment, Geronimo emerged from his hut, fierce looking in his war paint. He approached the five young warriors, and with a hard look in his shadowy eyes, he said to the group, "Why has Brondo gone to Fort Bowie?"

The young Apaches looked at each other with a bit of trepidation. Ramino, Brondo's closest friend, responded, "We cannot tell you, Geronimo."

A vicious scowl formed on Geronimo's dark face. "I demand that you tell me!"

Ramino shook his head, and then bowing it slightly, he touched the fingertips of his left hand to his forehead, the Apache sign of deepest respect. "Geronimo is a great Chiricahua warrior," Ramino said with feeling. "We hold him in the greatest of esteem. But our friend Brondo has trusted us with a secret. If we are to remain true to the Apache code, we cannot break Brondo's confidence."

Geronimo glared at Ramino with undisguised contempt and then swept the other four with the same hot glare. Wheeling, he headed for Cochise's lodge.

Clumin wiped a hand across his mouth and said, "There will be trouble now. Cochise will make us tell why Brondo has gone to the fort."

"No," said Ramino. "Cochise will respect the Apache code. He is not so rash as Geronimo. Cochise will wait until Brondo has returned and ask *him* why he went to the fort."

Cochise had just painted white stripes across his swarthy face and a yellow sunburst on his chest when he heard Geronimo's knock at his door. The chief went to the door and, with Arizpenora looking over his shoulder, heard Geronimo blurt out, "Cochise, your youngest son has ridden to Fort Bowie this morning."

Surprise registered in the eyes of the chief. "Are you sure?"

"I am sure," responded Geronimo. "I overheard Brondo's companions say so. I demanded that they tell me why he had gone to the fort, but they have refused to do so. Ramino says it is a secret between them."

Cochise, evidently disturbed, said, "I do not understand this."

"You can make them tell you," Geronimo insisted.

"I will not do that," replied Cochise flatly. "Since it is a secret between Brondo and his friends, I will not ask them to betray Brondo's confidence. You should know this."

The high-spirited Geronimo, who had little use for ceremony, snapped, "Why would Brondo be going to the fort?"

"I do not know," responded the virile chief, "but my son must have a good reason. I am sure he will tell me about it when he returns."

"And what if he is late in returning?" grunted the Chiricahuas's bloodiest warrior. "I remind you that all the ranches must be attacked at the same time so that no rancher can be forewarned of our approach. If Brondo is late, none of the ranches can be attacked. He must command his band. He is their leader."

Covering his own anxiety about the situation, Cochise held his face expressionless and said levelly, "My son will return in time."

At the same moment that Cochise was reassuring Geronimo, Colonel Brett Johnston was following Rayva and Brondo into the parlor. He was cursing under his breath, wondering how he had allowed this to happen. A hot knot formed in his stomach at the thought of Cochise's flesh and blood entering his home.

Brondo could not keep his thoughts off the half-breed woman's dazzling beauty. She had parted her long black hair in the middle and woven it into two thick braids, which were draped over her shoulders, dangling down the front of her body, almost reaching her waist.

Rayva stood barely an inch over five feet in height and weighed about a hundred and five pounds. Her slightly dark skin had a smooth, honey-cream complexion. She was dressed in a frilly white blouse, which emphasized her femininity, and the bright-red full skirt falling to just below her knees revealed her shapely calves and slender ankles. Brondo decided that the lines of her body were absolutely perfect.

Gesturing toward an overstuffed chair, Rayva said, "Please sit down, Brondo. I will get you some coffee." Looking at her father, who seemed rather off balance, she asked, "Would you like some coffee, Father?"

The colonel cleared his throat and said, "Uh . . . no, dear. No. I'll just sit here while you two drink it."

As the tall, silver-haired man eased onto a straight-backed chair, Brondo sat down in the chair Rayva offered him. This was his first experience with an overstuffed chair, and he appeared to be taken aback by sinking so far into it before it finally supported his weight.

The brunette woman returned from the kitchen bearing a tray with two steaming cups sitting in saucers. Brondo thanked her and reached for the cup closest to him. He obviously did not know what to do with the saucer, so he left it on the tray. Rayva smiled at his inexperience, sat down on a straight-backed chair facing him, and took cup and saucer in her hands. Brondo grinned sheepishly when he saw what the saucer was used for, but made no move to correct his error.

For a moment no one spoke. Brondo sipped at the hot coffee and studied Rayva's exquisite features. Certainly when the Great Spirit had formed her, He must have taken more time and greater care than usual. Every line and angle of her face was perfect, but most fascinating, even beyond her lovely mouth and finely formed brow, were those deep, expressive black eyes.

Brondo took a good look into the depths of those black eyes and was lost. Now he fully understood the feelings that had prodded his heart since yesterday—he had most certainly fallen in love. As his heart seemed to swell within his breast and drum his ribs, Brondo knew he had to have her.

Rayva, setting those vivid black eyes on the young man whose heart she had captured, said, "I can see that you are Apache, Brondo. Of which tribe are you?"

"I am Chiricahua." Brondo smiled.

Rayva looked at her father, who obviously did not want to leave her alone with Brondo. With a hint of irritation in her voice, she said, "Is there any army business that requires your attention, Father? You were about to leave when Trooper Akins knocked on the door."

Johnston adjusted himself uncomfortably on his chair. Scrubbing a palm across his face, he said, "Well, there's always something to do, honey, but I'm really in no hurry."

Rayva laughed softly in a way that sent a tingle spiraling down Brondo's spine. There was such a sweet, vibrant warmth about her. "Father," she said, "I am in no danger. Brondo risked his life yesterday to save me. He is not going to harm me today."

The colonel's face crimsoned, and every muscle in his body went taut. *She might as well learn the truth now,* he thought. Speaking his mind, he blurted, "Rayva, do you know who this young man is?"

Blinking her long lashes, Rayva asked, "What do you mean?"

Johnston held his daughter's eyes with a solid, steady glance. "You know who my greatest nemesis is, don't you?"

Nodding quickly, she said, "Cochise."

The colonel settled back in his chair as if his next words would be all that it took to drive Brondo from Rayva's life. "Well, the savage Apache that you are looking at right now is a son of Cochise."

Brondo stiffened, shifting his glance between father and daughter.

This time Rayva did not so much as blink. Speaking in a soft tone so as not to be offensive, she said, "May I remind you, Father, that I am half Apache? Does that make me a savage?"

Johnston cleared his throat nervously. "Well—"

"So Brondo is a son of Cochise," cut in the young black-haired woman. "That does not automatically make *him* your nemesis."

The tiny surface veins around Brett Johnston's eyes darkened and seemed to bulge. "Rayva," he said hoarsely, "you don't seem to understand. This young man—"

"Father," she cut in again, "can't you see that Brondo is different? He is not a mortal enemy of white people like his father. He didn't know I was half Apache when he risked himself to save me from a horrible death yesterday.

As far as he knew, he was risking his life for a white woman."

Brondo wanted to applaud her words, but he sat in silence, waiting to see if he was going to be ordered out of the fort. Yet he was troubled by her words, too, for they reminded him that later that day he would be expected to kill other whites when he raided the ranch that had been assigned to him. He dreaded not only the attack on the fifteen ranches but the repercussions that were sure to follow. He intended to do whatever he could to prevent the bloody raids from occurring, and it crossed his mind that revealing the well-orchestrated plans to Colonel Johnston would enable the ranchers to be evacuated. But he immediately rejected the idea; his loyalty to his father and his people was too great to do anything that might lead to their capture or annihilation. So the knowledge of the upcoming raids hung heavy in his mind.

There was a long pause. The colonel scratched at the back of his head while Rayva's words resounded through his brain. He looked at Brondo and then settled his gaze on his daughter. With the hint of a smile tugging at the corners of his mouth, he said, "Rayva, honey, you ought to become an attorney. You're a natural. You'd be the richest attorney in the country."

Rayva smiled at her father.

Turning to Brondo, the silver-haired commandant said, "Young man, I meant what I said yesterday. You saved Rayva's life, and for that I am in your debt. It's not right for me to assume that because your father is my mortal enemy, you are necessarily the same. What you did yesterday certainly shows that you are different."

Looking Johnston square in the eye, Brondo said, "I *am* an Apache, Colonel, and you understand that I must be true to my people. But I will tell you that I have talked with my father many times about the constant warfare between the Apache and the whites. I have tried to convince him to work at peaceful negotiation with you. All of this bloodshed is useless. So far I have gotten nowhere, but I will keep trying."

Johnston sighed, slapped his palms on his legs, and stood up. Brondo rose from his chair.

"Since you've come to see that Rayva is all right after her close call yesterday," said the colonel, "I'll let you two talk without my presence. I can see that she's in no danger. But I will ask that you stay only another twenty minutes."

As Brondo nodded his assent, Rayva rose, looked at the old grandfather clock in the corner, and said, "I will be leaving for Bowie in a half hour anyway, Father. If Brondo stayed much longer than twenty minutes, he'd be sitting here alone."

The colonel embraced his daughter, afforded the Apache a slim smile, and made his exit. Stepping off the porch, he gave the Appaloosa stallion an appreciative eye. As he crossed the compound, he saw Lieutenant Gary Donovan and nine men riding out of the fort. Assuming they were on a routine scouting mission, he proceeded toward his office.

As he drew near, Captain Hale Wilson came at him from his own quarters and said, "Colonel, may I speak to you for a moment?"

"Of course." Johnston smiled, halting.

"Just wanted to tell you, sir, that Betty is going to the sewing bee at Bowie."

"Good!" exclaimed the colonel. "That's a step in the right direction."

"Also, sir," said Hale, "I'm a little concerned that we're low on bedding and linens in view of the new troopers coming in. I caught it a couple of days ago in Corporal Skivington's report. I checked the inventory in the supply shack myself last night, and his count was correct. We're going to be short with a hundred new men moving in. Until we can get more, I'm afraid the new men may have to sleep in their bedrolls and share towels and washrags."

"I guess that won't kill them," chuckled Johnston. "They ought to be in here sometime today."

"They will be unless they've run into Indian trouble along the way, sir," Hale added. "Well, sir, I'd better go see Betty off. Thank you, sir."

The commandant saluted and then smiled as he watched Hale walk briskly toward his quarters. He was pleased that things seemed to be going better for the Wilsons and that he had been instrumental in the change.

In the colonel's quarters, Brondo set his hungry gaze on the lovely half-breed woman and asked, "Are you really all right after yesterday's ordeal?"

"I'm fine," she assured him with a warm smile. "And I'm glad you've come so I can express my gratitude for what you did. It was a very unselfish thing. Please know that I am thanking you from the depths of my heart."

Taking in her beauty like a dry sponge soaks in water, the handsome Indian said, "Miss Rayva, I would risk my life a million times to save yours."

Rayva's honey-cream complexion tinted.

"After I had the opportunity to meet you yesterday, I guessed that you had Apache blood in you," he said, changing the subject. "I find it interesting, with your father feeling as he does toward Apaches, that he was married to one."

"Oh, he wasn't married to an Apache," Rayva said quickly.

"No?"

"No. You see, the Johnstons adopted me. My mother was Apache. She . . . she was raped by a white man, and I was born as a result of the rape."

Flustered, Brondo said, "I am sorry. Please forgive my blundering. I—"

"It's all right, Brondo," she said sweetly. "There's no way you could have known." She went on to explain, "My mother was an Aravaipa Apache. The Aravaipas tolerated me in their midst until my mother died. I was four years old at the time of her death, and my mother's people then took me into the wilds of the Arizona desert and left me alone. I would have died if an army patrol had not found me. The leader of the patrol was Lieutenant Brett Johnston. He took me to the army camp near what is now Fort Huachuca. The Johnston's were childless, and they adopted me. That was sixteen years ago."

As they talked, Rayva and Brondo found that they thought very much alike. Rayva was particularly impressed with the way Brondo, as a child, had sought out and convinced an older member of the tribe to teach him to speak and read English so that he could better understand the new world in which his people lived. For his part, the young Apache felt his heart reaching toward the lovely half-breed, and while the conversation proceeded, he kept reading something in her eyes that seemed to be reaching toward him.

It seemed as if only a few minutes had passed when Rayva looked at the old grandfather clock and gasped, "Oh, Brondo, your time is up!"

Standing, he said softly, "Then I must go. I would not want to anger your father."

Rayva followed as the tall Apache moved toward the door. When he laid his hand on the knob, she said, "Brondo, once again please accept my thanks for saving my life."

Rayva was aware of the rise and fall of Brondo's powerful, muscular chest. Their eyes locked, and Rayva was finding it hard to breathe. As though in a trance, she moved closer to him, her ebony eyes fathomless and alluring.

Brondo felt himself being drawn into those inky depths and had no desire to resist. His heart was in his throat, but before he knew it, he was saying, "You are Apache. Do you know the tribal custom?"

A strange look appeared in Rayva's soft eyes. Breathing out the words in a husky whisper, she said, "You mean the custom that if a man saves the life of an unattached woman, she becomes his property?"

Smiling and fighting for breath, Brondo nodded wordlessly, and for lack of knowing what to do next, pulled the door open.

Rayva quickly pushed it shut, saying, "I like that custom."

Suddenly Brondo's whole world was in a whirl. He looked down at her, wanting to take her in his arms. Her lips soft and inviting, she tilted her face upward, and as he bent down, her arms encircled his neck. The sweet yearning within both of them brought their lips together in a tender, ecstatic kiss.

When he released her, she smiled and said, "Please come back and see me again. Soon."

"I will," Brondo answered, trying to make his lungs work properly. He stepped outside with his heart violently pounding his rib cage.

Colonel Brett Johnston was standing near Brondo's Appaloosa stallion when he saw the Apache emerge from his quarters. At the same moment Captain Hale Wilson returned, followed by a wagon bearing three women. After saluting, the two officers watched the wagon pull up in front of the colonel's quarters. Aboard were Sarah Benedict, the fortyish widow of Captain Dolph Benedict, who had been killed a few years previously; Elizabeth Simmons; and Betty Wilson, an insincere smile on her face. A dusty trooper sat on the front seat holding the reins.

As the wagon ground to a halt, Rayva darted through the door of the colonel's quarters past Brondo. The trooper on the seat started to climb down so he could help Rayva into the wagon, but Brondo moved swiftly toward the wagon and did the honors. Rayva, smiling at him as she settled in the seat next to Sarah Benedict, secretly squeezed the hand that had helped her in. Then she spoke cheerfully to the other women, surprised but pleased to see Betty Wilson.

Betty, still wearing her painted-on smile, wiggled her fingers at her husband. Hale smiled broadly and gave her a friendly wave.

As the wagon pulled away, Rayva waved at Brondo, and Brett Johnston scowled. He did not want her to get too friendly with him.

In less than thirty seconds the procession had passed from view. Brondo offered Johnston his hand, saying, "Thank you, Colonel, for allowing me to talk to your daughter. She is a lovely young lady."

Johnston nodded without comment. He wanted to tell Brondo never to see Rayva again but knew he couldn't since the Indian had so gallantly saved Rayva's life. He

silently hoped this visit would be the last and told himself
there should be no reason for Rayva and Brondo ever to
see each other again.

Changing the subject, the colonel ran his eyes over the
magnificent Appaloosa and said, "That's a beautiful animal, Brondo. I wish I had one like him."

Picking up his white-flagged rifle from where he had
leaned it against the porch, Brondo swung onto the stallion's back and said, "I am using him as a stud to produce
more of his kind."

Brondo was about to ask the colonel if he could come
back again to see Rayva when a corporal came running
from his post at the gate, shouting, "The new troops are
arriving, sir!"

Johnston and Hale turned their attention to the column
of blue-uniformed riders filing through the gate, and Brondo
quietly wheeled the Appaloosa and rode out. He was
stunned to see nearly a hundred soldiers in the column.
They were accompanied by several wagonloads of weapons
and ammunition, plus eight howitzer cannons mounted on
wheels.

Brondo thought of his father's plan to attack fifteen
ranches that very day. Digging his heels into the Appaloosa's ribs, he galloped like the wind for the Dragoons. He
had to warn Cochise about the bolstering of the troops at
Fort Bowie and of the firepower they were bringing in.

The bronze-skinned Apache guided the Appaloosa through
Apache Pass, knowing that if he rode at a good lope on the
long-legged stallion, he would be back at the Chiricahua
stronghold in the Dragoons in a little over an hour—plenty
of time to warn his father not to attack the ranches.

He allowed himself a moment to savor the sweet taste of
Rayva's lips on his own. He pictured the look in her dark
eyes just before they had kissed . . . and heard her say
again, *I like that custom. Please come back and see me
again. Soon.*

As Brondo reached the west end of Apache Pass, a mass
of blue uniforms on horseback charged out between two
huge boulders and converged on him. He was surrounded
instantly and forced to pull his mount to a halt. He was

facing nine ominous rifle muzzles, and it was obvious that
the men behind them meant business. A tenth man dismounted his horse and said in an insolent manner, "Going
somewhere, Apache scum?"

Brondo recognized Lieutenant Gary Donovan and fixed
him with an icy stare.

Eyeing the rifle in the Apache's hand with the white
flag on its tip, Donovan laughed. "Well, lookee there,
men! The Apache scum has already run up the white flag!
He's surrendering!"

The nine troopers echoed Donovan's laugh.

Holding out an empty hand, Donovan barked, "Give
me the rifle, Indian!"

Brondo hesitated briefly, but feeling the keen pressure
of the nine black muzzles, he relinquished his weapon into
the lieutenant's hand. Donovan handed the rifle to one of
the troopers and turned back in a sudden move, grasping
Brondo's ankle. Giving it a hard yank, he dislodged the
Indian, slamming him to the ground.

With the quickness of a cat Brondo was on his feet.
Before Donovan could react, the Indian drove a hissing
punch at him, connecting solidly on his mouth. The lieutenant staggered back but was caught with two more blows
before the soldiers could get off their horses and jump his
attacker.

Donovan sagged to the ground while three men went
for Brondo. The fleet-footed Apache seized the first one
and flipped him over his hip, causing the soldier to cart-
wheel and finally bounce in the dust. Brondo slammed the
next one with a rock-hard fist that sent him backward into
a patch of prickly pear cactus, the trooper screaming as
countless needles stabbed his backside. With the screams
ringing in the air, Brondo kicked the third trooper in the
groin, doubling him over.

Then, four other troopers pounced on the Apache and
flattened him on the ground. Brondo fought back hard,
but the four men wrestled him until he was lying facedown, helpless as his hands were bound behind him with
a rope.

When Gary Donovan got to his feet, assisted by two

men, his upper front teeth were loose and his mouth was oozing blood. His features were a deep red, almost purple, and he looked down at Brondo with murder in his eyes. Then his attention was drawn from the Indian by a trooper walking toward him with a water-soaked bandanna, which the trooper extended to him so he could wipe the blood from his face.

Donovan spit a mouthful of blood, accepted the bandanna, and dabbed gingerly at his lips. His hate-filled eyes were on the prostrate Apache again. Breathing heavily, he growled, "Get him on his feet!"

Brondo was jerked upward and placed on his feet, two husky soldiers holding him by the arms. Donovan handed the bandanna back to the trooper and stepped up close to Brondo, wrath blazing from his eyes as he said, "You listen good to me, Apache scum. Rayva belongs to me. Do you understand? I'm not going to allow a dirty, stinking Indian to get near her. Don't you ever even go near the fort again. You stay away from Rayva."

"Rayva has a mind of her own," Brondo said tonelessly.

Pounding his fist into his palm, the angry lieutenant breathed, "I'm going to give you a reason to stay away from her, *scum,* and I want you to think about it whenever you are tempted to see Rayva again."

With both fists clenched, Donovan moved in. The two big soldiers gripped Brondo's arms tight, but Brondo, quick as a cougar, used the soldiers as spring posts and brought up both feet and kicked Donovan violently in the face. Donovan's head snapped back from the blow, and he rolled in the dirt and then lay still, unconscious.

Brondo was trying to pull free from the two soldiers when three more jumped in and wrestled him to the ground. He was held there while the others gathered around Gary Donovan. A trooper came with a canteen and poured water on Donovan's face to revive him, and after several minutes Donovan was awake and sitting up, swearing vehemently. When his head stopped reeling, they helped him to stand up.

A burning paroxysm of hatred welled up in Donovan. His eyes squinted nearly shut as if he were sighting down a gun barrel. "Hold him!" he blared, charging at Brondo and kicking him savagely in the face. Swearing insanely, he kicked the Apache repeatedly in the head, chest, and stomach.

Brondo did not give his attacker the satisfaction of crying out or even grunting from the pain Donovan was inflicting upon him. The impact of the heavy boots against his body shot streamers of fire from head to toe, but he took it without a whimper.

When Gary Donovan had expended his strength, he stood over the Apache, gasping for breath and wiping blood from his own mouth. Eyes wild, he bellowed, "Now you're going to die, scum!"

At this Sergeant Harley Carter spoke up. "Lieutenant, I beg your pardon, sir, but you shouldn't kill him. He's Cochise's *son.* The whole Apache nation will go on the warpath if you kill him."

Donovan spit a mouthful of blood and sneered, saying, "Oh, I am not going to kill him, Sergeant. And this band of U.S. Army soldiers is not going to kill him, either."

Carter heaved a sigh of relief.

"But he *is* going to die, Sergeant!" hissed Donovan. "Mr. Brondo here is going to kill himself!"

Carter's face blanched. "What do you mean, sir?"

"Put him on his horse, men," Donovan said with a wave of his hand. "We're taking him to Rawhide."

"You mean the old mining camp?" asked the sergeant.

"Yeah," breathed Donovan with a vengeful glint in his eye. "That's exactly what I mean."

Brondo scowled at the lieutenant as he was hoisted onto the back of his Appaloosa, his hands bound tightly behind his back.

As his men were getting into their saddles, Donovan mounted his own horse and rode up to face Brondo. "You're going to kill yourself at Rawhide, scum. This is your last day on earth."

Chapter Eight

Lieutenant Gary Donovan and his nine men took their prisoner northward along the eastern edge of the Dragoon Mountains. Their eyes were peeled for any sign of Apaches. Along the way they paused in an arroyo long enough for one soldier to sneak onto a ranch and steal a lantern.

As they moved north Brondo watched the steady lift of the sun toward its apex in the brassy Arizona sky. He knew his father would be storming with fury when he did not show up in time to lead his men on the raid. He was not sure what Cochise would do in his absence. One of two things would happen: The Chiricahua chief would either appoint Ramino to take Brondo's place or he would abort the entire attack. Moving his lips as he prayed quietly, Brondo asked the Great Spirit for his father to do the latter. If the attack were made on the ranches as Cochise had planned, Colonel Brett Johnston would unleash his new forces on the Apaches. Fort Bowie was now nearly three hundred strong . . . and they had eight howitzers.

It was a half hour before noon when Donovan and his troopers rounded the north tip of the Dragoon Mountains and hauled up in front of a jumbled bunch of dilapidated old buildings. Looking around, Brondo remembered having seen the old mining camp as a boy. Even then it had been a ghost town. While the soldiers dismounted, his gaze fell on an old, weather-beaten sign, loosely hanging on a leaning post and swaying slightly in the breeze. The lettering on the sign was worn and faded, but he could make out the name Rawhide. Fifty yards to the rear of the tumbledown shacks was the mouth of the abandoned Rawhide Mine. The supporting timbers were badly weathered and sagged precariously.

When his feet touched ground, Lieutenant Gary Donovan barked at his men, "Get the Apache scum off his horse!"

The two husky troopers who had handled Brondo earlier now dragged him roughly off his Appaloosa and gripped him tight as Donovan explained his plan.

"There's a deep shaft about a hundred feet in from the mouth of that mine," said the lieutenant, pointing at it with his chin. "It goes down into the earth probably a thousand feet, and it's filled with water. The surface of the water is a little less than forty feet from the top of the shaft. Our Apache friend is going down that shaft."

Brondo felt a cold tingle dance down his spine. He glared hard at Donovan as the breeze plucked at his long black hair.

Sergeant Harley Carter spoke up. "Lieutenant, I don't like this too good. It's just plain cold-blooded murder."

An insidious grin curved Donovan's mouth. "Sergeant," he said, shaking his head, "it's not murder. I told you, the Apache scum is going to kill himself."

"But, sir," argued Carter, "whatever you're planning to do, it's still murder."

Donovan's eyes widened. Glaring stiffly at the sergeant, he said with clipped words, "Carter, let me get this straight. You, an enlisted man, are telling me, your lieutenant, that I don't know the difference between murder and suicide?"

Carter blanched and said, "Well, I—"

"How about the rest of you?" cut in Donovan, swinging his petulant glare at the others. "Do you know the difference?"

Sergeant Carter saw the majority of his fellow soldiers nodding their heads in agreement. Only one or two others seemed to have any conscience about what was going on,

but it was evident they were not going to act on it. The
sergeant knew he stood alone. It would be his word against
the others if he told this at the fort. Besides, the lieutenant was Colonel Johnston's fair-haired boy. Carter knew
he was defeated and might just as well go along with it.

Turning back to Carter, Donovan said, "Well, it looks
like you're the only uneducated man in this outfit, Sergeant. The rest of them know the difference between
murder and suicide. What's your problem, anyway?"

Carter dropped his head slightly. "I . . . I know the
difference, too, sir."

"Well!" Donovan said with a gusty breath. "It looks like
we can proceed without any more lip from you. Is that
correct?"

Brondo felt a knot form in his stomach as he heard
Carter answer meekly, "Yes, sir."

Within seconds Brondo was pushed into the dark, yawning cave as the soldiers followed their lieutenant. Donovan
carried two lengths of rope, and he gave Sergeant Harley
Carter the job of lighting and carrying the lantern.

By the light of the lantern, the soldiers moved cautiously back into the old mine. The scuffling of their feet
echoed hollowly along the rock walls of the dark cave. The
air grew noticeably cooler and dank. Brondo entertained
thoughts of wheeling about suddenly and making a run for
it, since the two troopers were now holding him rather
loosely. He knew, however, that he could never make it,
especially not with his hands tied behind him; the soldiers
would cut him down with their guns.

Abruptly the yellow ring of light showed them the shaft,
a hole about four feet in diameter. Extending some twelve
feet down from the top of the shaft was a rickety wooden
ladder, broken off at that point.

By the light of the lantern, Donovan tied one end of the
longer rope securely to the third rung of the ladder. One
of the men asked, "Why are you tying it down there,
Lieutenant? Why don't you tie it on the top rung?"

Cinching the triple knot tight with a grunt, Donovan
answered, "Just precautionary. It may take Mr. Brondo

some time to commit suicide. The chance of somebody
coming in here is slim, but if somebody does approach the
shaft, he could readily see a rope attached to the top rung.
With it down on the third rung it'll be hard to see. I sure
wouldn't want this Apache scum to be pulled out before
he kills himself."

Donovan let the loose end of the rope fall down into the
awesome black hole. Calling for Sergeant Carter to hold
the lantern over the shaft, he took note of how far the end
of the rope dangled from the dark water. "Ah!" he said
with elation while pulling up the rope. "Just the right
length. He'll be about six feet above the surface of the
water."

Finding a spot on the thirty-five-foot length of rope
some seven feet from the bottom end, the vengeful lieutenant used a sharp knife to saw more than halfway through
it, the cut strands of hemp fraying into a fan shape.

Chuckling fiendishly, Donovan said, "Have you boys
figured out what's happening here?"

There were some wordless grunts of affirmation. To
strike fear into Brondo's heart, Donovan decided to go
over it explicitly. "You see, Apache *scum*," he said with a
malicious leer, "I am going to tie you to the end of this
rope. Unfortunately, it seems to have been damaged severely in one place. Your weight pulling against the few
strands that are left intact will tend to pull them apart . . .
and the more you struggle," he said gleefully, "the faster
they'll break!"

Donovan moved closer to Brondo, who was still held by
the two muscular soldiers. His shadowed face looked eerie
and dreadful in the pale light of the lantern. "And struggle
you will, stinking savage! Because you're going to try to
get loose before all the strands break. By your struggling,
you'll rupture the remaining threads of rope and drop
yourself into the shaft. You'll commit suicide, Mr. Brondo!
You'll bury yourself in a watery grave!" He broke into
ghoulish laughter, its sound echoing through the murky
cave.

In the yellow light, Brondo's face went colorless, his
flesh turning cold as ice. Impulsively, he bolted from the

grasp of the two troopers and slammed Gary Donovan with his shoulder, the impact sending the lieutenant reeling into the black shaft. Donovan screamed as his fingers caught the clammy clay edge of the shaft, digging in like talons. As Carter and two or three others dropped to their knees to aid the lieutenant, Brondo was slammed against the uneven granite wall of the cave by the other troopers.

Carter had hastily set the lantern down near the edge of the shaft, and in its yellow light Donovan clawed wildly at the soft lip of the hole, screaming, "Help me! Help me!" In his fright, he could not find the ladder with his feet, which dangled helplessly beneath him.

Carter flattened himself on the floor of the cave and grasped one of Donovan's wrists and then the other. Shouting to the others, he said, "Grab my ankles! I've got him!" When he felt strong hands take hold of his ankles, he grunted, "Now pull!"

Within seconds, Gary Donovan was on solid ground, gasping for breath. He scrambled to his feet and moved to where the five troopers held the Apache, and his bulging eyes were riveted on the dark face of Brondo. His shadow made a menacing figure on the yellowed rock wall as he hissed, "I should have them just throw you down the hole, stinking savage! With those hands tied behind you, you'd drown in minutes! But you're not going to die that easily! I want you to hang there and think about the plunge you're going to take while the rope slowly unravels! I want you to sweat! I want you to feel death's cold breath on your dirty red skin before you drop!"

Donovan's fingers were trembling as he tied a four-foot length of rope around Brondo's slender waist and cinched it up tight. He checked the rope on Brondo's wrists behind his back to make sure it was still secure. Then he took the tail end of the long ruptured rope and quickly knotted it at Brondo's back to the rope around his waist. Using a large bandanna, he gagged Brondo securely.

"Okay," rasped the lieutenant with elation, "lower him down."

Brondo's body jackknifed, his head facing his knees, as he was eased down into the dark shaft. Sergeant Harley

Carter held the lantern over the edge of the hole so they could watch the Indian being lowered. With his face bent downward, Brondo could see the firelight from the lantern dancing on the surface of the black water below him. When the rope had been let out all the way and his weight tugged against it, the cut ends at the severed spot began to curl away from it.

Gary Donovan was like a child who had just won a game against a formidable opponent. His hollow laughter reverberated through the mine as he cried, "Good-bye, Apache scum! When you get to your happy hunting ground, remember that you sent yourself there! Go ahead, struggle! It's your funeral! I'll tell Rayva good-bye for you!"

Donovan and his men moved outside, blinking against the sudden glare of sunlight. The lieutenant's gaze settled on the big Appaloosa. "Well, my friends," he said gesturing toward the animal, "what are we going to do with our doomed Apache's horse?"

"We'd all like to have him, Lieutenant," spoke up one of the troopers. "But it would be a dead giveaway if we came ridin' him into the fort!"

There was a round of nervous laughter.

"There's only one thing we can do," said Donovan. "Turn him loose. If we kill him, he'll draw buzzards and lead the Apaches straight to him. We'll just remove his bridle and turn him loose. There's lots of wild horses about. He'll join one of the herds, and Cochise will never know what happened."

The soldiers agreed. The bridle was removed, and the Appaloosa was given a slap on the rump. He bounded away, soon passing from sight.

As Donovan and his men rode toward the fort, the lieutenant chuckled to himself. Rayva didn't know it, he was thinking, but she had seen the brave man who had saved her life for the last time.

Because of his position Brondo could not see up the shaft, but he heard Gary Donovan's laughter fade as the lieutenant walked away from the opening. Then the light disappeared, leaving him in darkness.

Brondo felt his body break out in a cold sweat. The awkward position he was in sent splinters of pain across his shoulders and down his spine. He fought to keep himself in control and not panic. As long as he was alive, there was hope.

The only thing he knew to do was to work his wrists against the prickly fibers of the rope until they began to bleed. Maybe the sticky moisture of the blood would make it possible to slip his hands free. It was going to take time, though, and there was no way of knowing how long the few strands of rope above him would last.

Keeping his body as still as possible, he twisted his wrists against the rope, and while he labored his mind went to Rayva. He must not die. He had read Rayva's love for him in her eyes . . . felt it in her tender kiss. They had a right to a life together, and they were going to have it. In spite of Gary Donovan. In spite of Colonel Johnston's hatred for Cochise. In spite of the predicament in which he now found himself.

As the rope chafed and cut into his wrists, he bit down hard on the gag between his teeth. The blood was slow in coming. Above his labored breathing Brondo could hear two distinct sounds—the lapping of the water against the grim walls of the shaft and the faint twang of the snapping strands of hemp.

Betty Wilson silently cursed the wagon carrying her to Bowie every time it jarred her body. She wished she were back home in Los Angeles. It was not yet midmorning, and the sun was already drying out the desert. Little puffs of dust were coming up through the cracks in the floor of the wagon, and a cloud of it hung low around the iron wheels.

While the other three women carried on a conversation, she let her eyes drift over the desert, hating every inch of it. At the moment the wagon was picking its way through twisted clumps of greasewood and dodging the tall saguaro cacti. The driver, in an attempt to shorten the miles between the fort and Bowie, had departed from the road, but Betty saw no beauty in Arizona's wild jumble of barren, craggy mountains, tangled thickets, rocky gulches, and sandstone pillars, which seemed to thrust themselves suddenly out of the desert floor.

Betty wondered why anyone would want to live in this grassless, sunbleached land with its maze of deep, jagged gorges and its labyrinth of colorless rocks and empty ravines. A chill shuddered down her spine as she caught sight of a diamondback rattler slithering under a large rock. Almost at the same moment a large dust devil picked up handfuls of gritty sand and threw it on her and the other occupants of the wagon.

The powder-faced blond woman unleashed a string of unladylike swear words as she spit grit from her mouth. The driver and soldiers riding close enough to hear her laughed. Sarah Benedict's mouth dropped open, and Elizabeth Simmons and Rayva Johnston ignored the outburst.

Conversation among the three women dropped off, and everyone rode in silence.

Rayva Johnston let her gaze settle on the mountains that were coming up on her right. Her mind drifted to Brondo and the few moments they had shared together that morning. She thought again of the kiss and the streamers of fire it had sent through her body. She had never experienced feelings toward any man like those she was having for Brondo.

As Bowie became a low, black smudge on the desert horizon to the north, Betty Wilson noticed a small stream of water spilling out of a dark cleft in a high granite shelf they were passing. The clear water pooled in a circular formation of low-lying rocks. For a moment she pictured the Los Angeles beach with its swaying palm trees and foamy white shoreline. Again she promised herself that somehow she would escape this bleached-out prison and return to Los Angeles.

Elizabeth Simmons was sitting next to her, and Betty looked at her out of the corner of her eye, studying her profile. How foolish Elizabeth was to trust Don! With Don

Simmons now in the forefront of her mind, Betty pondered his trip to California and drooled over the hundred thousand dollar payroll he would be escorting

Her thoughts were in a whirl. She racked her brain, trying to think of a way she could get away from Fort Bowie forever and at the same time get her hands on that money. She knew Don was crazy about her, but she seriously doubted that he would take her and abscond with the payroll.

Bowie, Arizona, lay baking in the midmorning heat as the wagon and its escort pulled into town. Betty took note of the shops and stores along Main Street and counted four saloons among them. When the wagon came to a stop in front of the town hall, she cast a dull glance at the women gathered in front of the place and braced herself for a boring day. Then, as she was alighting from the wagon, her eyes happened to stray across the street to the Pink Palace Saloon and Casino.

There were several men loitering in the shade of the Pink Palace's long, low porch, their attention on the Fort Bowie women and the mounted escort of blue-uniformed men. Suddenly Betty Wilson spotted a familiar face. She did a double take, not believing her eyes, but it *was* Red Stoker's blocky build and unmistakable red hair. A cigarette dangled characteristically from the corner of his mouth.

Red Stoker recognized Betty at the same instant. He grinned, threw his cigarette down, and started toward her. Quickly Betty used her eyes to tell him to stay away. Shifting them toward the saloon, she conveyed the message. Stoker understood. He should go inside and wait for her. Unnoticed by the other women or the soldiers, he nodded and vanished through the dark door of the Pink Palace.

As the women were chatting and filing into the town hall, Betty turned to Rayva Johnston and said, "I spotted a couple of shops up the street that I would like to visit. I'll join you in a little while."

The lovely half-breed smiled and said, "All right, Betty. I'll introduce you to the ladies when you come back."

Betty Wilson moved slowly along the boardwalk, pre-

tending to look in shop windows while the soldiers headed
for a shady spot farther down the street. When they had
passed from view, she dashed across the dusty street and
headed for the Pink Palace. The men who loitered in the
shade of the porch gave her an appreciative look as she
drew near. Smiling at them, she said cheerfully, "Good
morning, gentlemen!" and then pushed through the swinging doors.

The inside of the saloon was cool and quite dark. It took
Betty's eyes a few seconds to adjust, having come from the
glare of the brilliant sunlight.

"Over here, Betty!" called Red Stoker, standing up at
the table where he had been sitting, situated in the far-
thest corner of the saloon.

Betty threaded her way among the tables toward Stoker.
A few other patrons were scattered about.

"Red!" she said excitedly. "It's so good to see you!"

The thick-bodied outlaw folded her into his arms, and
they embraced for a long moment and then enjoyed a
brief kiss. He pulled out a chair for her, and as she sat
down Betty looked around to see if any of the other
patrons were within earshot. She decided that if she and
Stoker spoke low, no one would hear their conversation. A
scheme was already taking shape in her mind.

Before being seated, Stoker called toward the bar, "Hey,
Jack! Bring my lady friend a glass of sherry!"

Betty giggled. "Red . . . you remembered!"

Sitting down and pouring himself a shot glass full of
whiskey from a bottle on the table, he grinned and said,
"Honey, how could I ever forget? We had a lot of good
times together, you and me." Studying her face in the dim
light, he sighed, "You're more beautiful than ever."

Enjoying the compliment, Betty looked at him long-
ingly and said, "We did have some good times, didn't we,
darling?"

Stoker took a gulp of whiskey. "We could've had a lot
more if you had accepted my marriage proposal."

Betty's eyes dropped downward. She let the following
few seconds of silence speak eloquently for her, then lifted
her gaze slowly. "That was a mistake, darling," she said in

a sad tone. "How well I know it now. I could have had six years of wedded bliss with you."

"I haven't been in Los Angeles since you turned me down," Stoker said wistfully. "Too many memories."

Reaching across the table, Betty took hold of his hand. She started to speak when the bartender drew up and set a glass of sherry in front of her. Smiling at the man, she said, "Thank you." When he was gone, she gripped Stoker's hand and breathed, "I've missed you, Red. What have you been doing with yourself?"

Betty was hoping that Red Stoker had not changed. He had lived and operated outside the law nearly all of his life. A plan had formed in her mind, and if he was still an outlaw, she was sure he would gladly be a part of it.

"Nothin' new," he answered in a dead tone.

"You mean you're still hitting a bank or a stagecoach now and then?"

"Yeah. It's a livin'. How about you? I heard you married an army officer."

Letting go of Stoker's hand and easing back in the chair, Betty took a sip of her sherry and sighed. "Yeah. And I'm miserable. He's stationed at Fort Bowie, so I'm there with him. It's horrible, Red. Just horrible."

"You're not happy with your marriage, I take it."

Rolling her eyes, she said, "Oh, you are so right." Taking another sip of her drink, she batted her long eyelashes against her fraudulent tears and choked out the words, "I've got to get out, Red! I mean now. I've got to get away from my husband, the army, the fort, and Arizona. If I don't, I'm going to lose my mind!"

Stoker leaned forward and half whispered, "You still have some spark for me in your heart?"

Putting a dreamy look in her blue eyes, Betty lied, "Not just a spark, darling. The whole flame is still there! I'm still in love with you, Red. There hasn't been a day in these six years that I haven't rued the moment I sent you away. I've thought of you constantly—I've wanted to be in your arms again, but there was no way to find you."

Stoker took Betty's hand in his own. "I'll take you back

to Los Angeles if you'll go with me. But I want you to divorce your husband and marry me."

Putting her face close to his, Betty smiled. "Of course, darling."

She watched Red Stoker draw a deep breath of her spicy perfume and sigh. Then, bending her face even closer, she brushed her lips against his. Holding his captivated eyes with her own, she said, "How would you like to have me, plus a hundred thousand dollars to share between us?"

Stoker's amber-flecked eyes shone with eagerness. He showed his crooked teeth in a broad smile. "Betty, honey, what man in his right mind could turn down a deal like that? Tell me more."

It warmed her to see Stoker jump at her offer. "Well," she began, "I happen to know that a lieutenant from Fort Bowie is going to carry a one hundred thousand dollar payroll to California on the stagecoach that's coming through day after tomorrow."

Stoker eyed her skeptically. "And how do you happen to know that?"

Easing back in her chair, Betty adjusted herself nervously and replied, "Well, I . . . uh . . . I've been seeing the lieutenant on the sly." Hastily she added, "Things are just so dull around that old fort, Red. But Don Simmons means nothing to me—absolutely nothing. He's just a way of eliminating boredom."

Stoker's smile was gone.

Reaching across the table, Betty squeezed his hand and said softly, "Red Stoker is *my* kind of man. You're the one I love, Red—you always have been. I'll divorce Hale, darling. I want to marry you."

Betty watched her charm do its usual melting job. Finally the thick-bodied outlaw smiled and said, "Okay, honey. It's you and me."

Leaning across the table, she kissed him. With the light of avarice gleaming in her eyes and her mind whirling, she said, "Here's the way it will work. I'll get myself booked on the stage and board it with Don Simmons at the Apache Pass station just outside of Fort Bowie."

"Just like that?" Stoker asked. "What will your husband say?"

Betty giggled, taking another sip of sherry. "Don't worry about Hale. I have him wrapped around my little finger. He knows I'm lonely and bored here, so I'll tell him I want to get away . . . maybe to visit my sister in Los Angeles. He'll go along with it, no questions asked."

Stoker nodded in agreement.

"Then," she proceeded, "you book yourself on the same stage and board it at the Dragoon Springs station."

"Okay," he said. "Keep talkin'."

Betty thought for a long moment and then said, "We'll check the route ahead of time to find a secluded spot for getting rid of the other passengers—we'll have to shoot everybody on board. I figure we can make it look like a robbery. We'll ditch the money somewhere nearby and pick it up later, after we've had a chance to report the robbery. Then after things quiet down, we'll grab the next stage for California and be on our way!"

A light flickered in Stoker's evil eyes. "Tell you what, babe." He grinned. "There's an old mining camp about two and a half miles from Dragoon Springs along the edge of the Dragoon Mountains. We can pull it off there and hide the money inside the mine. It's the perfect spot."

Greed danced in Betty's eyes. Soon she would hold the hundred thousand dollars in her own little hands.

Proceeding, Stoker said, "We'll make it look like Apaches ambushed the stage, and nobody'll think otherwise. The Apaches seem to be on the prowl right now. I saw them wipe out a band of white men recently."

Betty smiled.

"To make it look real," Stoker went on, "we'll have to nick ourselves with a couple of bullets. We'll stumble into Dragoon Springs and tell them we're the only survivors. Afterward I'll lie low, while you go back to the fort until things calm down. Then you'll catch the stage to California again, I'll join you, and we'll disappear with the money."

"It'll be worth the loss of a little blood," she said.

Looking deep into her blue eyes, Red Stoker asked, "It

doesn't bother you to murder this Don Simmons guy? Or the rest of the passengers and crew, for that matter?"

Giggling like a schoolgirl, Betty responded without feeling, saying "How else can we ever get our hands on a hundred thousand dollars? Your plan is foolproof, darling. All the blame will fall on the Apaches."

"Can you get a revolver?" asked Stoker.

"Yes." She nodded, adding, "Hale has several around our quarters."

"You'll need to carry it on board the stage in your handbag. We'll have to play it by ear once we're on the stage, but one of us will have to drill the driver and shotgunner first." Stoker squinted his eyes. "You're sure you can do it—blow three or four people into eternity, I mean."

Betty's greed covered her like a hard finish. Without emotion, she said, "I can do it."

"Okay." He nodded, amazed at her coolness.

Pushing her chair back, she said, "I have to be going now. I'm due at a stinking hen party." Standing up, she added, "I'll see you when you board the stage in Dragoon Springs."

Skirts swishing, Betty weaved around the tables and headed for the swinging doors. Red Stoker smiled to himself and poured the shot glass full of whiskey.

The Arizona sun blazed a fiery path to its peak in the sky, drawing from the land the last remaining moisture left by the previous day's rain. As Cochise paced back and forth in front of his adobe lodge, where Mangas and his warriors waited patiently amid the war-painted Chiricahuas, a scowl creased his forehead.

Mixed emotions stirred within him. He was worried that something might have happened to Brondo, yet ready to be angry with him if he did not have a good reason for being late.

Geronimo, unlike the others, was impatient. Speaking up from where he sat on an old wooden crate near Cochise's door, he said, "Enough of this waiting! Something must be wrong, Cochise. It is not like Brondo to be late. I say we take two hundred warriors and ride to the fort. If they are holding him, we will storm the gates and set him free."

Halting to look down at Geronimo, Cochise said, "No. A full-scale battle could result from a show of force like that. Here on our ground we could withstand such a battle, but not on their ground. I will take twelve warriors and ride to the fort under a white flag."

Geronimo was about to protest when a shout was heard, and Cochise turned to see Brondo's big Appaloosa trotting in riderless, its coat shiny with sweat. The magnificent animal came to a dusty stop, nickering at the other horses, which stood idly by. Dark Apache eyes immediately took note that the bridle was missing, suggesting foul play. Geronimo put it into words. "Look, Cochise!" he said, pointing. "The horse has no bridle! Brondo has met up with someone who means him no good."

Without comment the worried Cochise stepped up to the Appaloosa, running a hand over its back and looking it over. "There is no blood," he commented audibly. "Someone has taken Brondo captive, setting his horse free."

Geronimo, always ready for a fight, uttered a deep guttural exclamation. "The soldier coats have captured your son, Cochise! Now are you ready to show force? Let us take *all* our warriors and those of Mangas. We will tear the fort apart and bring Brondo back!"

Cochise was not yet ready to risk the lives of many warriors by launching an attack on Fort Bowie. He wished he knew why Brondo had gone to the fort. Glancing at Brondo's five companions, who stood in the group squinting against the glare of the noonday sun, he wanted to ask them to break confidence and tell him Brondo's secret, but he could not bring himself to do it.

Shaking his head at Geronimo, he said, "I will not go into war with the soldiers at Fort Bowie until I am sure they have captured or harmed my son. I will take twelve warriors and ride to the fort. I will make further decisions when I know what has happened to Brondo."

His dark features filled with malignity toward white

men, Geronimo uttered something to himself, swung a fist through the air, and returned to the wooden crate. Moments later, he and the others watched as Cochise and the chosen twelve warriors rode out of the camp.

Chapter Nine

Inside the mine shaft, Brondo heard the hemp threads snapping above him one at a time. Though his wrists were oozing with blood, the rope binding them still held them tight. Grunting through his nose and past the gag in his mouth, he worked feverishly to loosen his bonds.

Periodically Brondo's thoughts flicked to Rayva, but he forced them back to his predicament, knowing that he had to concentrate on escaping if he wanted to see her again.

He could hear the hungry water lapping beneath him, and the occasional ping of the breaking strands of the rope taunted him. He had confronted death many times in battle, but never in his twenty-three years had he faced it in such a helpless position.

Pain racked his body; the joints and muscles that were being strained by his unnatural position cried out for relief. In spite of the headband he wore, salty sweat ran into his eyes, burning them. His bleeding wrists felt as though they were banded with red-hot irons.

Suddenly he felt the rope give, as if most of the remaining strands had broken. A cold claw of fear squeezed his heart. He bit down hard on the bandanna, tensing his jaw, preparing to fall into the cold black water. He felt another tug at the rope around his waist, but then nothing more; the long rope held firm. It was then he realized that the knot up above, where the rope was tied to the ladder rung, had slipped. He let out a sigh of relief through his nostrils.

But the motion created by the slipping knot above had put more stress on the few strands that still held Brondo's weight. He heard several snap at the same time and knew not many could be left. Time was running out.

As he pulled violently against the rope that held his wrists behind his back, he suddenly felt the heel of his left hand slide against that of his right. The rope had loosened! A faint glimmer of hope rekindled itself in Brondo's heart.

More strands were breaking, but Brondo was able to move his hands. In less than a minute more his left hand came completely out of the rope. He was free!

Cautiously he reached one hand behind him until he felt the long rope from which he was suspended. Taking the rope in his bloody hand, he pulled himself around so that he was facing up and, grasping the rope with both hands, began to climb it, hand over hand. If he could just get past the place where Donovan had cut it . . .

Twice he slipped back a few inches because of the blood on his hands. The hemp strands continued to pop. Gripping the rope harder, he made his way upward, sucking hard through his nose for air. At last his right hand touched the frayed place where the rope had been cut and moved above it, barely brushing the thin threads that still held together, and he took hold of the comforting thickness of the rope above. Breathing a prayer of thanks, he continued upward, hoping that the knot that had slipped on the ladder would not give way now.

Within moments he reached the top and, using the ladder to boost himself, bellied over the edge. Catching his breath, he detected a faint light coming from the mouth of the mine a hundred feet in the distance.

With another prayer of thanks to the Great Spirit for sparing his life, Brondo untied the gag and spit it out. Pulling gulps of breath into his lungs, he removed the long rope from the one around his waist and dropped it to the ground.

Still wearing the shorter rope around his waist, Brondo made his way toward the sunlight at the mouth of the cave. Pausing for a few minutes in the deep shade of the cave's mouth, he let his eyes adjust slowly to the glare. Still squinting, he moved out of the mine, looking around for his horse. He knew they would not dare ride into the fort with the Appaloosa, but when he could find no sign of it, he feared they might have taken it to some secluded spot and killed it.

Determining which direction would take him into the depths of the Dragoons, Brondo headed for the Chiricahua camp.

Lieutenant Gary Donovan and his men drew near Fort Bowie early in the afternoon. Speaking quietly, Donovan said, "Now, men, we all have the story straight, don't we? I got these cuts and bruises on my face when my horse shied at a rattler and threw me."

The nine men in blue agreed to back the lieutenant in his story. Sergeant Harley Carter was feeling bad about Brondo's horrible fate, but nothing about the truth of it would ever come from his mouth.

The fort gates were opened to allow the scouting patrol to enter, and the squad dispersed. Gary Donovan went immediately to the post physician to have his facial cuts treated and to see if anything could be done about his loose teeth.

Two hours later a corporal knocked at the door of Colonel Brett Johnston's office. The colonel, deep in thought as he pored over important government papers he had recently received in the mail, looked up from behind his desk and said, "Come in!"

When Corporal Ed Shoney pushed the door open and stepped inside, Johnston took one look at his face and knew that something was awry. "What is it, Shoney?" he asked before the corporal could speak.

"Sir," Shoney replied, almost with a gulp, "we've got a strange situation out at the gate."

Leaning forward, the silver-haired commandant said, "Well, what is it, man? Speak up."

"Well, sir," said Shoney, clearing his throat nervously, "it's Cochise."

Johnston's thick eyebrows arched as he stood up and echoed, *Cochise!*

"Yes, sir." The corporal nodded, and as his superior officer moved around to the front of the desk, he went on to explain, "He's got a dozen warriors with him. They approached the gate under a white flag. Cochise is asking to see you."

Colonel Brett Johnston scratched his head. Looking at the floor, he mumbled, "What on earth could he be doing here under a white flag asking to see me?"

"What's that, sir?" asked Shoney.

Lifting his head up, Johnston said, "Uh . . . well, uh . . . bring the Apaches inside the fort, Corporal. Park them out there on the parade ground and usher Cochise to my office."

"Yes, sir," said the corporal, saluting. He pivoted and was gone.

Brett Johnston rubbed his chin as he returned to his desk and sat down. This was going to be strange indeed. The two men had never met under civilized circumstances, only on the battlefield while each commanded his troops. Their hatred for each other had been born in an atmosphere of powder smoke, blood, and death.

The knock at his office door less than five minutes later caused the colonel's stomach to lurch. He called for the corporal to open it, and Ed Shoney appeared in the doorway, followed by Cochise. Johnston, behind his desk, rose.

"You may see the colonel now, Chief," said Shoney, gesturing and then stepping out on the porch.

Cochise stepped into the office, his tall, straight shape silhouetted against the bright glare of the sun coming through the doorway. On the parade ground beyond, Johnston could see his men surrounding the other dozen Apaches, who remained on their horses.

For a moment there was silence. Brett Johnston had to struggle to conceal the hostility he felt toward the Apache leader. Cochise locked the colonel viselike with his black eyes.

"Come in, Chief," Johnston finally said, making an attempt at being cordial. "Would you like to sit down?"

Cochise's muscular frame moved inside the office, and he said in his deep voice, "I will sit, Colonel."

Remaining on his feet, Johnston said, "What did you want to see me about?"

"It is about my son, Brondo," Cochise said levelly. "Has he been to the fort today?"

"Yes." The colonel nodded. "He was here early this morning."

"He has not yet returned to our camp," responded the stalwart chief. "His horse returned riderless with its bridle missing just past noon, the time he was due back. It is apparent something has happened to Brondo."

Reading Cochise's dark, expressive eyes, Johnston said, "And you figured that *we* might have detained your son."

Without batting an eye, the Indian said, "Yes. Apaches and whites are mortal enemies, Colonel."

Looking Cochise straight in the eye, Brett Johnston said, "You have my word on it, Chief. We have not detained your son. No one in this fort would harm a hair of his head on a personal basis. On the battlefield, yes, but not in a personal conflict on the grounds of this fort."

Puzzlement showed in Cochise's eyes. "And why is this?"

It was the colonel's turn to look puzzled. "You don't know why Brondo came here this morning?"

"My son is a man, Colonel. He does not have to inform me as to where he is at all times, nor of what he is doing."

Eyeing the chief carefully, Johnston asked, "Am I to assume that you do not know of Brondo's heroic act yesterday?"

"I have been told nothing," Cochise said flatly.

Johnston found it odd that neither Brondo nor his companions had made Brondo's brave deed known in the Apache camp. "Chief," he said with a hint of a smile, "your son saved my daughter from a horrible death yesterday at the risk of his own life. We are still at odds with you and your people, but young Brondo is a bit of a hero in this fort."

Surprised, the venerable chief said, "I would like to hear about it."

Colonel Brett Johnston took five minutes and told Cochise the story in detail. As Cochise listened, he grew a bit miffed that his son would save the life of a white person, especially at the risk of his own life, but secretly he was proud to have a son who had the courage to do what Brondo had done.

"I can understand your concern for Brondo's whereabouts at this time, Chief," said Johnston, "but we have not seen him since he rode out of here this morning."

Cochise had no doubt that the colonel was telling him the truth. "May I ask, Colonel," he said, "what was Brondo's business here this morning?"

"He came to see Rayva. Said he wanted to make sure she was all right after yesterday's harrowing ordeal. He stayed about half an hour and then left."

"If you please, Colonel," said Cochise, "would you allow me to speak to your daughter? Possibly Brondo mentioned to her where he was going."

"I would be happy to let you talk to her if she were here," said Johnston. "However, Rayva is away and will not return for a few hours."

"Perhaps you have had some patrols out that have returned," said the worried chief. "One of them might have seen Brondo."

"There are two patrols still out," Johnston replied. "But one has returned. I'll have the patrol leader brought here immediately, and we'll see if they saw anything."

Lieutenant Gary Donovan was summoned. As he entered the colonel's office, Johnston eyed his bandaged face and said, "Lieutenant Donovan, I heard about your accident. Are you all right?"

"Doc says I'll be fine," answered Donovan trying to smile past swollen lips. His eyes moved to the Apache chief, who stood near the door.

"This is Cochise, Lieutenant," said Johnston, nodding toward the Indian. "His son, Brondo, seems to be missing. I was wondering if you and your men saw any sign of him while you were on patrol."

"No, sir," lied Donovan. "I'd know him, too. That Appaloosa of his would stand out anywhere."

Johnston dismissed Donovan. As soon as he had gone, Cochise said, "Colonel, you owe me nothing, and if you do not grant the favor I am about to ask you, I will understand."

Johnston held his gaze, waiting for the favor to be expressed.

"May I leave a man here at the fort to question your daughter when she returns? She might be able to give some clue as to Brondo's whereabouts."

Reading the concern in Cochise's eyes, Brett Johnston overlooked their standing as enemies and, feeling for Cochise as a father, granted the request. Cochise left a warrior named Morano at the fort and rode out, worry scratching at his mind.

Brondo, his face swollen and his ribs sore from the beating Lieutenant Gary Donovan had given him, walked painfully toward the Apache camp. As he made his way along the rugged path, his anger toward Donovan increased until a burning desire to kill the soldier with his bare hands grew within him . . . not in an act of murder but in a man-to-man confrontation.

But even as he entertained such a notion, Brondo knew that if he challenged Donovan on the basis of what the lieutenant had done to him, he would probably never get to see Rayva again. Certainly none of the soldiers who had been with Donovan would admit that they had left him to die in that dark shaft, dangling from a rope. It would be his word against theirs. There was no question that Colonel Johnston would take the word of his lieutenant and his soldiers over that of an Apache.

The love that Brondo found in his heart for the beautiful young half-breed was stronger than his hatred for Gary Donovan. He would have to forget what Donovan had done to him.

Twice Brondo stopped at small streams in the Dragoons

to soak his scabbing wrists in cool water. Even slight movements of his fingers stabbed his wrists with pain.

Soon he reached the Apache settlement, and as he plodded wearily into view of his people, they rushed to him, elated to see that, though battered and bruised, he was alive. Encircling Brondo, the Chiricahuas began asking what had happened. Nachise and Naiche moved in close, along with Geronimo. On their heels were Ramino, Clumin, Eskamin, Bisilo, and Zenta.

Brondo had caught sight of his Appaloosa in the rope corral and was looking thoughtfully toward the animal as Nachise pressed him for an explanation.

Gazing at Cochise's lodge, Brondo spoke past swollen lips, "I will tell the story to our father. If he wants it known to the tribe, he may tell it."

"Our father is not here," said Nachise advisedly. "He has taken a band of warriors and has gone to the fort looking for you."

"How did he know I was going to the fort?" queried Brondo.

"I told him," spoke Geronimo. "I overheard your five companions discussing your ride to the fort."

Brondo's dark eyes flashed to the faces of his friends.

"Please do not be angry with them," said Geronimo. "They did not know I was listening, and they have not divulged your reason for going there."

Brondo nodded, his swollen lips showing a slight smile. His five friends smiled back.

Brondo thought about his father being at the fort. No doubt Cochise would learn from Colonel Johnston about Brondo saving Rayva's life. He was not sure how his father would take it. Apaches were supposed to kill whites, not save their lives.

Running his gaze over the crowd, Brondo saw that Mangas and his Mimbres were still present, along with the majority of the Chiricahua warriors who were supposed to be in camp at the time. This meant that the fifteen ranches had not been attacked. He was relieved. Now he would have a chance to talk to his father about the new troops that had been brought in to Fort Bowie . . .

and the eight howitzers. *In fact,* he thought, *Cochise will probably see them for himself while he is at the fort.*

At that moment Brondo's eye caught sight of his mother standing in the doorway of Cochise's lodge. Apache women were supposed to remain in the background, so Arizpenora had not approached her son.

Speaking to the crowd around him, Brondo said, "And now I must bathe this dirty body." With that, he pulled away from them and headed toward his mother.

Arizpenora embraced him with tears in her eyes. "I am so glad you are all right," she told him. "I will hear what happened to you when you tell your father."

Ramino, Clumin, Eskamin, Bisilo, and Zenta accompanied Brondo as he took fresh clothing and went to a nearby stream to bathe his black-and-blue body. Since he had stated that he wanted to tell the story of the incident only to his father, they did not inquire what happened to him. After bathing, Brondo applied salve made from the yucca plant to his wrists. He was seated on the ground in front of his own hut, talking with his companions, when he heard excited voices and looked up to see his father and the eleven warriors returning.

Cochise's eyes lit up when he saw Brondo rise and move toward him. Sliding from his horse, the chief stepped close to his third son and took hold of his upper arms, looking at his swollen face. Cochise's brow furrowed. "I am glad you are alive, my son," he said with relief in his voice. "What happened to you?"

Brondo was reluctant to tell his short-tempered father the truth, but absolute fidelity was the code of the Apache. "May we talk in your lodge, Father?" he asked.

Inside the lodge, Arizpenora sat in a corner and listened while Brondo told his story, beginning with his rescue of Rayva and then following with his reason for visiting the fort. From there, he told Cochise of Lieutenant Gary Donovan and his men beating him and leaving him in the mine shaft to die.

When Brondo had finished the story, Cochise's dark features had gone almost black. His eyes burned bitterly as his temper boiled. Standing up, he swung a fist through the air and hissed, "Donovan and his wicked men will die!"

Rising to look his father in the eye, Brondo said, "My father, may I explain something to you?"

Regarding his son with his smoldering eyes, he said calmly, "Yes."

"I must first ask if you are angry with me for saving Rayva's life."

The chief rubbed his chin. "When the colonel first told me about it, I was angry. But I also felt pride run through my blood. It was a brave thing to do, my son."

Relieved, Brondo glanced quickly at his mother and then said to Cochise, "My father, we have always talked straight as the barrel of a rifle to each other."

"Yes."

"Do not ask me why, but I have fallen in love with Rayva."

Cochise's square-honed features instantly registered a different anger from the one he felt a moment ago. A storm brewed in his dark eyes. "My son is in love with a *white woman*?" he bellowed.

Arizpenora's hand went to her mouth.

"*Half* white woman," corrected Brondo.

"The colonel's daughter is a half-breed?" asked Cochise.

"Yes, my father."

"What kind of Indian?"

"Apache."

The fire in Cochise's eyes began to fade. "Apache?"

"Yes. Colonel Johnston and his wife adopted her when she was very small. Rayva's Apache mother was raped by a white man. When Rayva's mother died, the Aravaipas took the child into the desert and left her to die. The colonel, who was a lieutenant then, found her and took her home."

Studying his son's puffy, handsome face, Cochise said, "You met this half-breed maiden only yesterday, and already you are in love with her?"

Again Brondo flicked a glance at his mother, perhaps looking for moral support, and then said to Cochise, "Yes. I told you not to ask me to explain the workings of my heart. But I know how I feel."

Tilting his head to look at Brondo from the tops of his eyes, Cochise queried, "And how does the half-breed feel toward Brondo?"

"She has not put it into words, Father," he replied carefully, "but the love is there. I saw it in her eyes."

"This is quite sudden," Cochise said in a flat tone. "Can you and this half-breed woman really be in love?"

Before Brondo could voice a reply, Arizpenora spoke up, "My honorable husband, may I say something?"

The lovely Arizpenora was the delight of Cochise's heart. Allowing her a warm smile, he said, "Of course."

"When Arizpenora fell in love with the handsome Cochise, it happened in less than a minute."

Moving to her, he tenderly stroked her face, and then he turned to Brondo and said, "Your father will agree that it is possible to fall in love quickly. No one but Brondo can know his heart." Cochise's eyes clouded again as he added, "But if the army does not punish the guilty soldiers who tried to kill Cochise's son, the Chiricahuas will!"

Brondo reasoned with his father, pointing out that if he caused trouble over the incident, Rayva would be out of his life forever. He explained that Gary Donovan's purpose in wanting to kill him was to get him away from Rayva, for Donovan was in love with her also. But Brondo knew Rayva was not in love with Donovan; she had asked Brondo to come back and see her very soon.

Cochise's wrath slowly cooled as Brondo's words took hold, emphasizing his deep feeling for Rayva Johnston. His temper in check, he looked at his love-struck son and said, "As your father, Brondo, I must help you to face one cold, hard fact."

"Yes?" responded Brondo.

"The colonel will never consent to his daughter marrying an Indian. He is white, and he thinks white. He is at war with the Apaches."

"But Rayva is half Apache," argued Brondo.

"But *you* are more than Apache," Cochise said evenly. "You are a son of Cochise. There is bitter blood between Colonel Brett Johnston and Cochise."

"But you can negotiate an end to this bitter strife," countered Brondo. "Besides, Rayva has a mind of her

own. Under white men's laws, she will be of age in another year."

"Of age or not," said Cochise, "the colonel will do all in
his power to keep a relationship from developing between
you and his daughter. Especially a marriage."

"Not if there were peace between you and the colonel,"
said Brondo.

Cochise laid a hand on his son's muscular shoulder.
"The only way there will be peace between Cochise and
the colonel is when the colonel and all his white soldiers
get off Apache land forever."

Brondo bit down on his lip.

"I will do this much for you, my son," said Cochise. "I
will not declare full-scale war because of what Donovan
and his soldier coats did to you. But our conflict with the
whites continues. The ranches will be attacked tomorrow."

Brondo immediately told his father of the reinforcements that had arrived that morning at Fort Bowie. Cochise
said he had noticed an abnormal number of horses in the
corrals but had not seen the men.

"Did you see the eight new cannons?" asked Brondo.

"I did not," responded Cochsie.

"My father, if we attack the ranches, the soldiers will
come at us with those cannons. They can launch shells to
the very spot where we now stand. You must reconsider
your plan to make war on the ranches."

The mention of cannons caused bitter memories for
Cochise. In his mind's eye, he recalled the debacle at
Apache Pass on July 14, 1862, when the bluecoat army
brought the deadly howitzers firing twelve-pound canis-
ters and almost wiped out the Chiricahuas.

Since that time, Cochise had not attempted a mass
action. To fight back at the whites over the past ten years,
he had sent out small war parties to attack wagon trains,
miners, prospectors, and settlers on remote ranches. But
the continual influx of whites had brought him to the point
of wanting to wipe them out in larger numbers.

Brondo's words took effect in Cochise's mind. Coupled with
those words and the bitter memory of the howitzers, Cochise
decided to carry on his warfare in the same way he had been

doing for a decade. Looking at his son, he said, "Brondo speaks with the wisdom of a gray-haired man. It is my decision to continue Chiricahua warfare as it has been done for these many years. We will not attack all the ranches at once."

Brondo would rather have heard that Cochise was going to negotiate a peace treaty with the whites, but he was greatly relieved that there would not be a wholesale attack on the ranches. The army seemed unwilling to engage in full-scale war over random raids, and this was at least a step in the right direction.

After returning that evening to Fort Bowie, Rayva Johnston was visibly shaken when she learned that Brondo was missing. Morano had approached and questioned her about the Apache before she had even alighted from the wagon. While the other women were climbing down, Rayva said with deep concern, "It was my understanding, Morano, that Brondo intended to return to the Apache camp when he left here this morning. Oh, I do hope nothing has happened to him."

In the crowd of soldiers that gathered around the wagon was Lieutenant Gary Donovan. A wave of anger washed through him when he saw Morano question Rayva and heard her concern over Brondo's absence. Pushing his way to the wagon, Donovan quickly offered his hand to Rayva, helping her from the wagon. He hated the worry that was evident in her eyes.

As her feet touched the ground, Morano mounted his pinto and said softly to her, "Thank you just the same, Miss Rayva."

Donovan had taken her hand, but Rayva pulled it loose now and said to Morano, "Please let me know as soon as there is any word of him."

Gary Donovan watched Morano ride out of the fort, and he smiled to himself. The ignorant Apaches would never find their beloved Brondo. He was in a watery grave by now, never to be seen again. No one was going to come between Donovan and Rayva.

Nearby, Betty Wilson stepped down from the wagon

and moved among the crowd of soldiers until she spotted
Lieutenant Don Simmons. Making her way toward him, she
found a brief moment to speak privately to him, telling him
to come and see her as soon as possible. Hardly had she
given Simmons the message when she saw Hale coming
across the compound. Hurriedly she headed for her husband.

Smiling at Hale, she said demurely, "Hello, darling!
Did you miss me?"

Smiling back with an affirmative nod, Hale threw an arm
around Betty's slender waist and began walking her toward
their quarters. "Did you enjoy the sewing bee?" he asked.

"Oh, yes, darling," she lied. "It was quite enjoyable."

When they had moved inside their quarters and closed
the door, Betty kissed her husband with feigned passion
and said, "Hale, I'm glad you encouraged me to go today.
This little excursion has revealed something to me."

"Another kiss, then you can tell me about it," he said,
bringing his lips down on hers. Releasing her, he asked,
"Now what is this great revelation?"

"Well, darling," she began, "getting away from the fort
for a little while today made me realize how very cooped
up I've been feeling, and that, I believe, was the reason
for all the . . . the trouble I've caused you. I think if I
could get away for a little while, I would find life here at
the fort more tolerable." Pouting seductively, she said,
"Do you understand what your foolish wife means?"

Captivated by her deep-blue eyes, Hale said, "I think
so, honey. Where would you like to go?"

"Los Angeles."

"Los Angeles?"

"Yes, to visit my sister Joan. Just for a couple of weeks.
Will you let me go?"

Taking the luscious blonde in his arms, he replied, "If it
will make you happy . . . and make our marriage sweeter,
of course I'll let you go."

Betty smiled and kissed him warmly.

When their lips parted, Hale said, "I'll go to the station
first thing tomorrow morning and book you a seat. There's
a stage coming through day after tomorrow."

He began to press his lips against hers again, but she

gently pushed him back and said, "Hale, honey . . . would you mind doing it today? I want to make sure that I get a seat." She put her arms around his neck and pulled his face to hers before he could answer.

After a long, impassioned kiss, he whispered, "I'll do it now, honey. But I want to pick up where we left off when I get back."

When Hale Wilson had left for the Butterfield station just outside the fort, Betty went to the bedroom to get into more comfortable clothes. She tossed her bonnet on the bed, sat down, and was just removing her shoes when there was a tap on the window. Turning about, she recognized the face of Don Simmons. Dashing to the window, she threw it open. Simmons crawled through and took her into his arms, and she kissed him warmly.

"I saw him leave, honey," said Simmons. "You said to come as soon as possible."

"He'll be back shortly," Betty told him, "but I thought you might like to know that I will be riding with you on the stage to California."

Simmons was elated. He asked her how she had managed to set it up. When she explained how she had subtly coerced her husband, Simmons's eyes lit up. "Betty," he said, "I have an idea."

"What is it?" she asked with a lilt in her voice.

"Now's our chance, honey! If you're willing, when we get to California, we'll abscond with the hundred thousand dollars and go to Mexico! We'll live the rest of our lives like a king and queen!"

Though amazed that Simmons was willing to become a thief and an army deserter to have her, Betty was also pleased. She cared nothing for him, of course, and she was not interested in becoming a fugitive or in living in Mexico. But leading the foolish man on, she said, "Oh, darling! It sounds wonderful! I'm with you all the way!"

Elated beyond words, Don Simmons kissed Hale Wilson's wife and crawled back out the window.

Moments later, Hale returned with Betty's ticket. The stagecoach was scheduled to leave the Apache Pass station at nine-thirty in the morning, the day after next.

Chapter Ten

Arriving at the Apache camp in the Dragoons just after dark, Morano, immediately learning of Brondo's safe return, went directly to the campfire in the middle of the settlement. There Cochise, his three sons, and several warriors were gathered, sitting on the ground. Happy to see Brondo alive, Morano told him that Rayva was deeply concerned for him and was anxiously awaiting word of his safe arrival.

Thrilled that Rayva had so openly spoken of her concern for him, and wanting to see her again, Brondo stood up and said, "I must ride to Fort Bowie immediately and let Rayva see that I am all right."

Cochise also rose. "And what are you going to tell her, my son? That the lieutenant tried to kill you so there would be no competition for her hand? This could stir up trouble you do not want."

Holding the chief's gaze with his own, Brondo rebutted him, saying, "My father, the noble Cochise, has taught me since childhood to be honest. I will tell Rayva the truth but ask her not to tell her father. Donovan and his men would only deny the charge."

Cochise, seeing that his son would not be deterred, said to Brondo, "You are going to ride to Fort Bowie tonight, it is clear. But I will not let you go alone. Take your warriors with you. Lieutenant Donovan might try to kill you again."

The young Apache agreed, and moments later he rode

out of the Dragoons accompanied by Ramino, Clumin, Eskamin, Bisilo, and Zenta.

A few hours later, when the six riders moved into the circle of light made by the large lanterns that sat by the gate atop the fort's wall, they saw one of the two sentries jump up and grab his rifle. Brondo, aboard his Appaloosa, looked to make sure that the white flag on Ramino's rifle was easily seen.

"Halt!" called the sentry. "Who are you and what do you want?"

"I am Brondo of the Chiricahuas. Miss Rayva Johnston is awaiting word of my well-being. I have come to see her."

"You'll have to come back in the morning," the sentry said in a gruff manner. "The colonel is not present to grant permission."

"Miss Rayva will grant permission," responded Brondo. "If she knows I am at the gate, she will want to see me."

The two sentries were from among the new reinforcements and knew nothing of Brondo's heroic deed in saving Rayva Johnston's life. "Why would an Apache be that important to the colonel's daughter?" asked one of them.

"You will find out if I have to tell her later that I was at the gate and you refused to inform her," Brondo said coldly.

The two sentries whispered to each other; then one of them disappeared. "He'll be back in a moment," said the other one.

When Rayva Johnston heard the knock at the door of the colonel's quarters, she laid down the book she was reading, rose, and stretched. Opening the door, her eyes fell on the unfamiliar face of the sentry.

"Miss Rayva," he said, "I'm beggin' your pardon, but there's a pesky Apache out at the gate who insists on seeing you now. I told him it would be best for him to come back in the morning, but he talked like you would have my hide if I turned him away."

Rayva's eyes lit up. "Is his name Brondo?"

"Yes, ma'am."

Smiling gleefully, she said, "I certainly would have your

hide if you turned him away! Bring him in here right away."

Rayva stood in the doorway, her heart pounding, and watched as the sentry returned to the gate. Then Brondo started walking across the well-lit compound while his companions waited just inside the gate, holding his horse.

Tears touched the lovely young woman's cheeks as Brondo approached. Happiness and love danced in her dark eyes as she stepped off the porch and walked toward him. "Brondo!" she exclaimed. "You're all right!"

Silently the Apache closed the gap between them, the yellow lantern light exposing his swollen features.

"What happened to you?" Rayva asked, moving close to him and thumbing away her tears.

"I will explain it if you have time to see me," he said, looking down into her captivating face.

"Of course." She nodded. "Please come in."

In the colonel's quarters Rayva closed the door and moved close to Brondo, who towered over her. He saw compassion in her fathomless eyes as she examined his cuts and bruises. His arms ached to hold her, but he made no move to do so.

She lifted a hand and lightly ran her fingertips over some of the swollen places. "You poor dear," she said. "How did this happen to you?"

Without speaking, the Apache lifted a hand and tenderly took hold of hers.

"Oh, Brondo!" she suddenly gasped upon seeing the purple scabs that were forming on his wrist. Quickly she looked at the other wrist and gasped again. "At first I thought you had fallen or something, but now I can see that your wrists were bound . . . and . . . and you were beaten, weren't you? Brondo, who did this awful thing to you?"

Still holding her hand, he said, "I will tell you about it, Rayva, if you will promise to keep to yourself what you are about to hear."

"I promise," she said without hesitation.

"The sentry said your father is not here. When do you expect him?"

"Not for at least two or three hours," she responded. "He's gone into Bowie to see some friends."

"All right," he said. "May we sit down?"

"Of course."

The young couple sat down at the kitchen table. Rayva offered to make him coffee, but Brondo told her his lips were too sore to drink it. She listened intently as Brondo told her of Gary Donovan's attempt to kill him.

As Brondo had walked through the compound toward Rayva, several soldiers had been moving about. Two, walking together, were Sergeant Harley Carter and Corporal Fred Bates, both of whom had been in the group that had put Brondo in the mine shaft.

"Hey, Sarge!" said Bates excitedly. "Do you see what I see?"

Following Bates's pointing finger, Carter set his eyes on the young couple in front of the colonel's quarters. When the sergeant recognized Brondo, he breathed a secret sigh of relief. Somehow the resourceful Apache had freed himself from his death trap.

"Donovan's got to hear about this!" said Bates, and in a flash he was gone.

While Rayva was learning of the torture Brondo had endured, Bates was dashing into the single officers' quarters, where Gary Donovan was playing poker with three other officers. Bates said breathlessly, "Lieutenant, I need to see you in private!"

Speaking around the cigarillo between his teeth, Donovan kept his eyes on the cards in his hands and said, "Don't bother me now, Bates. I'm busy."

"Lieutenant, this is very important. I need to talk to you in private *now*!"

Disgustedly, the muscular lieutenant slapped his cards down on the table and stood up. "Gentlemen," he said to the other officers, who were looking at the corporal with annoyance, "I will return shortly. If any of you sneak a look at that hand, I'll drive nails through your eyeballs."

Donovan's card-playing friends snickered. As the two

men headed for the door. Donovan said malevolently, "This better be important, Bates!"

Outside in the dark shadows, Fred Bates looked around to see if anyone was within earshot. Men were milling about in the light of the many lanterns on the compound, but no one was close enough to hear their conversation, and seeing this, Bates blurted out, "Lieutenant, we should have done something else with that Apache. He didn't die in that mine shaft."

Gary Donovan looked at the corporal's face as if it had just turned green. Lancing Bates with a cold stare, he said, "Would you say that one more time?"

Bates choked on the words. "Brondo is not dead!"

Donovan's face twisted in disbelief. Eyes flaring, he seized the corporal by the shirt and pulled him so close that their noses were almost touching. "What do you mean, that Apache scum isn't dead?"

"I just saw him! Both of us did, Carter and me!"

"Where?"

"Over at the colonel's quarters."

"The colonel isn't there. . . . You mean that the scum is in there with Rayva?"

"Yes, sir. I saw them go inside."

Gary Donovan swore vehemently and headed across the compound.

"That dirty skunk has no claim on me!" Rayva Johnston hissed when Brondo told her of the lieutenant's attempt to kill him. Slamming the table with her fist, she said, "I know I must keep my word to you, but I sure would like to tell that scaly-bellied snake what I think of him!"

Pushing back his chair, Brondo said, "Rayva, I must be going."

She rose with Brondo and reached out her hand, touching his arm. "I am so glad you are all right," she said softly.

Brondo's heart thundered against his ribs. Laying a hand on hers, he took a deep breath and said, "Rayva, I cannot keep it inside me any longer. I love you. I love you like I have never loved anyone before."

In tender response the beautiful half-breed moved closer to him and said in a velvet tone, "I cannot hold it within me any longer, either. I love *you*, Brondo. I must give you my heart."

Brondo's chest seemed to explode as he folded her into his arms. They stood there for a long moment, holding each other, letting their heartbeats blend. Finally they moved to arm's length and looked into each other's eyes. "I want to kiss you," he said in a whisper, "but these lips are in pretty bad shape."

Looking up at him with adoring eyes, Rayva smiled and then raised up on her tiptoes. Tenderly she touched her sweet lips to his. Then a serious look framed her perfectly formed face. "You know my father will fight this relationship," she said ruefully.

Nodding, he replied, "Yes. I expect that. But somehow this love we have between us will win out."

"Yes," she agreed. "It may take some time, but our love will win out."

Brondo embraced her again, saying, "I will come back and see you again . . . as soon as I can."

"Make it very soon, my darling," she cooed. As he moved outside, she whispered, "Good night," and closed the door behind him.

His blood pumping fast and warm, Brondo was walking along the edge of the buildings toward the gate when suddenly a dark form stepped from the shadows into his path. He halted, recognizing Gary Donovan.

Brondo stood in silence, hating the man who had appeared before him like some formidable beast.

Through clenched teeth, Donovan said, "I don't know how you got out of that shaft, *scum*, but there's more than one way to skin a cat. You stay away from my woman or you're a dead man."

Standing like a granite column in the dim light, Brondo felt his cheeks turn hot with anger. Responding tonelessly, he said in his deep voice, "If the lieutenant with the yellow belly owns a woman, Brondo has never met her."

Donovan's eyes bulged, becoming wild. "I'm gonna kill you, scum!" he rasped.

"In order to do that," said the Apache, his black eyes boring into Donovan, "the cowardly lieutenant will have to come after Brondo with a band of men. He is too timid to face Brondo alone."

For a long moment, Lieutenant Gary Donovan glared at Brondo. Then he licked his lips nervously, but still he said nothing.

A slight smile tugged at the corners of Brondo's swollen mouth. Walking smoothly past Donovan, he said dryly, "Just as I thought. The lieutenant is brave only when in the company of his men."

Gary Donovan's whole body was shaking with fury as Brondo mounted the big Appaloosa and rode out of the fort with his five companions.

Through quivering lips, Donovan hissed, "You're a dead man, Apache scum. Do you hear? *A dead man!*"

On the following morning Cochise gathered his group leaders together to make plans for attacking the new ranches one at a time over a period of several weeks. Geronimo spoke up, arguing that the Apaches should wipe them out in one sweep as originally planned, but Cochise reminded him that Fort Bowie had just added a hundred troops and eight cannons. The other forts in the area may have bolstered their numbers and weapons also. Sporadic hit-and-run attacks would draw less animosity from the army than a sweeping assault, he explained, yet would still take their toll, frightening some ranchers away and making others think twice before settling in the area.

Cochise then reminded the group leaders, his sons included, of the particular ranches they were to demolish, and he scheduled the one Brondo had been assigned first. Brondo was to take his five warriors and wipe out the ranch the next day, killing everyone on the ranch and burning the buildings.

Brondo spoke up and told his father that he would go into battle against the soldiers any time it was necessary, but he would not attack defenseless ranchers or women and children.

"They are trespassing on our land!" Cochise snapped in anger.

"We have been over this many times before, my father," Brondo said calmly. "We can wipe out these ranchers, but whether you want to believe it or not, others will come to take their place. The more whites we kill, the more troops and guns they will bring in. I love our land as much as any Apache loves it, but I know that we are hopelessly outnumbered. I repeat what I have said many times in the past. It is in our best interest to negotiate peace with the whites."

Cochise knew, as did his other two sons, that there was wisdom in Brondo's words, but his stubbornness prevailed. Reluctantly he relieved Brondo and his five warriors from attacking any ranches, telling Brondo instead to take his men to Apache Pass and appear at the Butterfield station when the stagecoach came through the next morning. They were not to attack this one but just let the whites see that the Apaches were watching. The scheme was to make them nervous.

Relieved that his father would not pressure him to kill ranchers and their families, Brondo agreed.

The bright-red Abbott and Downing stagecoach was parked in front of the Butterfield station house at nine-twenty the next morning, and the agent was hooking up the fresh team of horses to it. Driver Wally Forbes and shotgunner Hec Allen were loading baggage. Several people were standing around the coach, including three passengers.

All eyes were suddenly drawn to the band of Apaches that came riding up, fear registering in the faces of the small crowd. The six Apaches reined in at the water trough, dismounted, and let their horses drink.

The young shotgunner up on top of the stage looked down at Wally Forbes, who was handing him a suitcase, and whispered nervously, "Wally, I think those Apaches are plannin' to attack us!"

Forbes released the suitcase into Hec Allen's hand and said, "Don't worry about them, Hec. I know those Indians. What they're doin' is only a ploy to make us nervous."

"I hope you're right," whispered Allen, wiping his hand shakily across his mouth.

"If they were gonna attack," said Forbes, "they'd come from ambush. This is just Cochise's scare tactic. Best thing to do is ignore 'em."

Allen's gaze whipped to the Indians. "Is one of them Cochise?"

"Naw," said the wizened old driver, grinning. "I'm sure the top dog has better things to do. That one with all the muscles is his son, though."

"Yeah?"

"Mmm-hmm. Name's Brondo. And he's as tough as he looks."

At that moment Captain Hale Wilson, paying the Indians no mind, pulled up in a wagon, his beautiful wife seated beside him. The captain helped her down and ushered her to the stagecoach. Betty, casting a fearful glance at the Apaches, said, "Hale, what are the Indians doing here? Will they attack the stage?"

"No, honey," he assured her. "When they come out in the open like that, it's just their way of harassing us. They'll ride away when the stage pulls out."

"What's to keep them from following us and attacking the stage out on the road?"

"Nothing," responded Hale, "but it wouldn't be like them to do it that way."

"Who's to say what those savages will do?" she said, taking hold of Hale's arm.

Another army wagon pulled in, driven by a trooper and occupied by Lieutenant Don Simmons. In his hand Simmons had a common-looking suitcase, which contained two canvas bags. The one hundred thousand dollar payroll was inside. After the lieutenant jumped from the wagon, he sauntered to the stagecoach and handed the suitcase to Hec Allen to be placed in the boot. At that instant Simmons caught Betty's eye, and with his own told her the suitcase contained the money.

Betty kissed her husband good-bye, thanking him for letting her go visit her sister, and entered the stagecoach. While the other passengers were boarding, she looked out the window beside her seat, and in clear view were two of Brondo's companions, Ramino and Zenta. Her mind clicking, she made a mental note of their description.

Zenta wore an old Derby hat and a blue denim vest with silver studs. Ramino was smiling at someone Betty could not see, and she noted that his front teeth were missing. Unlike most of the Apaches, Ramino's nose was flat. His hair was in a single pigtail, and he wore a necklace made from a diamondback rattler.

Don Simmons greeted Captain Hale Wilson and climbed into the coach. As he sat down directly across from the highly perfumed blond woman, they cast furtive glances at each other. Betty clutched her handbag tightly, feeling the weight of the .44 caliber revolver inside.

The other passengers were Mr. and Mrs. John Clendon, who had boarded the stage in New Mexico, and Sergeant David McFleary, who had just retired from the army. He was leaving Fort Bowie for Tucson.

Hale Wilson spoke a few kind words to McFleary, thanking him for his faithful service to the U.S. Army and wishing him luck. He told Betty good-bye one more time and returned to his wagon.

As the stage pulled away, Betty threw a kiss to Hale and took a long look at Ramino and Zenta. She got a quick glance at the other Apaches at the water trough but was not able to see them clearly.

She smiled as she saw the fort's walls for what she hoped would be one of the last times.

At Fort Bowie, Lieutenant Gary Donovan was crossing the sunbleached compound when he caught sight of Rayva Johnston coming out of the sutler's store. Changing his course, he headed toward her. Rayva saw him coming and wished she could detour around him. Since it would not be possible, she stiffened for the encounter. For the sake of her promise to Brondo, she would be cordial to Donovan, but no more than that.

"Good morning, beautiful!" Donovan said, smiling and tipping his hat.

Rayva turned a pair of cool eyes on the man. Nodding, she said, "Good morning, Lieutenant Donovan."

"*Lieutenant Donovan?*" he echoed. "Is that any way to greet the man you're going to marry?"

"What book of fiction did you read that in?" she clipped.

Donovan looked at her with shocked amazement in his eyes. "Fiction?"

"Yes, fiction," she replied flatly. "Gary, I might as well tell you this straight out, so there won't be any further question about it. I am not in love with you, and I am not going to marry you."

With sudden irritation Donovan snarled, "You're in love with that stinking Apache, aren't you?"

"It's none of your business who I'm in love with," she said curtly. "Besides, Lieutenant Donovan, you seem to forget that I am half Apache. If you married me, you would have to put up with the stink!"

Neither of the two saw the approach of Colonel Brett Johnston, who was now in earshot.

Angrily, Donovan snapped, "If you marry Brondo, you'll double stink!"

Rayva swung her palm and violently slapped the lieutenant's face. His head rebounded, and he was about to give Rayva a slap in retaliation when he caught sight of the colonel. Wheeling, he walked away briskly, even more determined to kill Brondo.

Johnston eyed the diminishing figure for a moment and then turned to his daughter. Worry was in his eyes as he asked, "Aren't things going well between you two?"

"You might as well know, Father," she said rubbing her hand. "I'm not in love with Gary, and marrying him is out of the question."

Johnston looked back to the spot where he had last seen Donovan and then queried, "What did he mean by saying if you marry Brondo, you will double stink?"

Rayva paused for a moment, swallowed hard, and replied, "I'm in love with Brondo, Father. And he is in love with me."

The colonel looked as if he had been hit in the stomach with a battering ram. "We've got to talk about this now," he said with a shaky voice. "Let's go to my quarters."

They sat down in the colonel's quarters, and the old man was about to speak when Rayva took hold of his hand. Looking at him tenderly, she said, "Father, words can't express how much I appreciate what you and Mother have done for me. No one ever had better parents. But I'm an individual; I must live my own life. No one can dictate which man I'm to fall in love with."

Fixing her with a stare that combined hurt with anger, he lashed out, "Brondo is a savage!"

Still holding his hand, speaking softly, Rayva said, "Brondo is *not* a savage. He's kind and gentle and quite cultured for his background. He's educated himself by reading many books."

Johnston's lips were pale, but his face was flushed. "Any son of Cochise is a savage!" he spewed harshly. "You are not to see him again. Do you hear me?"

Rayva's face pinched as Johnston quickly rose. "Father, please!" she begged, also rising. "You must give Brondo a chance to—"

But the furious colonel stormed out, swearing loudly and slamming the door with a bang. Heartbroken, Rayva stumbled to an overstuffed chair, collapsed into it, and sobbed.

Chapter Eleven

When the stagecoach rolled into Dragoon Springs, Betty Wilson was relieved to see Red Stoker, his thick frame leaning against the outside wall of the station. He was smoking a cigarillo.

The passengers alighted and headed for the privies. Telling Dora Clendon to go first, Betty nonchalantly wandered near the spot where the heavyset redheaded man leaned against the wall. The agent was just coming out the door, and Betty asked him where she could get a drink of water. He pointed a thumb over his shoulder, saying that there was a bucket of water and a dipper inside.

Stoker followed her in. They had only a moment alone, but in that time he told her the signal he would give when it was time for them to start shooting passengers and crew. He would light a cigarillo, take three puffs, and throw it out the window. At that instant, they would shoot.

Stoker had counted four passengers other than themselves. He instructed Betty to sit in a corner, and he would sit across from her in the far corner on the other side of the coach. That way each of them would be in a position to kill the two passengers on the bench across from them. When Betty said she had been sitting on the right-hand side, facing forward, Stoker said she must take the same seat. After she had shot her two people, she was to aim for where the shotgunner would be sitting outside and hit him, firing through the roof of the coach. Stoker said he would take care of the driver.

Betty Wilson, cold and calculating because of her greed, assured the outlaw that she would handle her part. They left the station house before the other passengers returned from the privies, making sure that no one saw them together.

Twenty minutes later the passengers were moving toward the stage to board. Red Stoker jumped in ahead of everyone else to be sure of getting the seat he wanted. Sergeant David McFleary and Lieutenant Don Simmons looked at each other upon seeing the new passenger's impolite move. Then they shrugged their shoulders and grinned.

When all the passengers were seated, the outlaw Stoker introduced himself as Red Smith. He was riding backward, with Sergeant McFleary to his left and Lieutenant Don Simmons sitting beyond McFleary. Directly across from Simmons was a steady-eyed Betty Wilson, playing to a tee her part as Simmons's secret lover. To Betty's immediate left was Dora Clendon, and to Dora's left, across from Red Stoker, was John Clendon.

The bright-red Concord coach rolled out of Dragoon Springs. Betty knew from Stoker's description of the Rawhide mine that the ride would be short. As the wheels of the stage settled into a steady whine her nerves began to tighten. Don Simmons caught her eye and smiled. The cold-blooded woman smiled back, thinking that Don would not be smiling at her if he knew she was going to kill him in a few minutes.

Dora Clendon tried to take up conversation with Betty, but the blonde remained politely silent. Her attention was on Red Stoker, who was looking out his window. Dragoon Springs soon passed from sight, and he was watching for familiar landmarks that would tell him they were nearing Rawhide.

The next three minutes seemed like an eternity to Betty, but suddenly she saw Stoker move a hand to his shirt pocket. A warm tingle fluttered down her spine as slowly she reached inside her handbag, gripped the revolver, and quietly thumbed back the hammer. She glanced up and saw that Don Simmons was smiling at her again, obviously unaware of what her hand was doing and probably thinking of the life he and she were going to have together in Mexico.

Red Stoker's right hand now rested on the butt of his holstered revolver. With his left hand, he carefully placed the cigarillo in his mouth and then fished in his shirt pocket for a match. Betty felt her nerves screw down a little tighter. She was aware of David McFleary saying something to John Clendon, but the words were lost in her excitement.

Stoker flashed the match with his thumbnail, touched the flame to the tip of the cigarillo, and took a deep pull, drawing smoke into his lungs. Betty's gaze briefly flicked to Sergeant McFleary. She would shoot him first. The fool Simmons would be next.

Stoker calmly flipped the match out the window, sat back, and began to smoke, looking out the window as he did. After taking two long drags on the cigarillo, he turned toward Betty. His eyes riveted on hers, he brought the cigarillo to his lips for the last draw, inhaled deeply, and then, exhaling, reached with his left hand for the open window. Betty watched with a mixture of fear and excitement as he flipped the cigarillo out the window.

On cue Betty whipped out the .44, aimed it at McFleary's chest, and fired. The impact of the slug caused him to grunt heavily before he jerked back and then folded forward.

Stoker's gun was out, blasting away at the Clendons. There was a shout from up in the box, and the stage started to slow down.

The blonde's eyes turned on Don Simmons in a cold, icy glance. The black muzzle swung on his chest, and for a brief moment time seemed to stand still. The knowledge that he had been betrayed and was about to die registered painfully in his bulging eyes, and his face went white. He stared at Betty through the blue-white smoke in wild, helpless terror.

The gun bucked in Betty's hand, sending a bullet to explode the lieutenant's heart. Simmons had not fully slumped over before Betty fired twice through the roof, aiming the deadly .44 at the spot where Hec Allen was seated in the box above.

Red Stoker had the door open as the coach came to a halt. Swinging out, he hung on to the doorframe with his left hand while aiming the revolver at Wally Forbes with his right. "Get it stopped!" he shouted at Forbes.

The elderly driver jerked hard on the reins, hollering at the team to stop. As Stoker's feet touched ground, Forbes, who had seen his partner keel over, cried, "Don't shoot me, mister! Please! I—"

The outlaw smiled cold-bloodedly and squeezed the trigger. Wally Forbes jerked as the bullet entered his body, and then he peeled off the coach and hit the ground with a thud. The horses were whinnying nervously.

Having jumped out her door on the opposite side of the coach, Betty looked up at the young shotgunner, who was hanging over the edge of the box. Blood was foaming at the corners of his mouth. She had put two bullets in him, but he was still breathing. As she moved close, Allen beheld her with bleak, glassy eyes. Knowing she had one bullet left, Betty eared back the hammer and lifted the muzzle in line with Allen's forehead. The shotgunner made a little grunting noise and closed his eyes. The .44 roared, its report echoing across the vast, empty desert.

Quickly the murderers pulled from the boot the suitcase containing the payroll. Betty dropped to her knees and opened the suitcase and then yanked out the two canvas bags. Stoker helped her open one of them, and they began to laugh, growing hysterically mirthful with their riches.

Finally closing the suitcase, they went to work. While Betty opened the other pieces of luggage and scattered the contents all around, Stoker dragged the bodies from the coach and strewed them about the area.

Pulling his gun, Stoker said to Betty, "I'm gonna kill one of the lead horses so the team can't pull the stage away."

Nodding, she said, "You got a sharp knife on you?"

Giving her a blank look, he said, "Yeah. It's only a pocketknife, but it's plenty sharp. Why?"

Regarding him impassively, she said, "We're supposed to make this look like Apache work, aren't we?"

"Yeah."

"Well, don't Apaches scalp their victims?"

Red Stoker's face blanched. He had not thought of that. "Yes, they do," he said weakly.

While Stoker shot the left lead horse through the head, Betty cut the forelock from Don Simmons's scalp. Stoker's stomach flipped over as he saw her carrying the bloody scalp and moving to the body of Dora Clendon. Within minutes, the icy-hearted woman had scalped all of the victims.

Reloading their guns three times, Stoker and Betty walked a circle around the stagecoach, firing bullets into it from every angle, trying to make it look as though Indians had attacked in ambush. The horses, still in harness, were unable to charge away in their fright because of the one dead horse on the ground.

The pair ran past the old, faded Rawhide sign and entered the mouth of the mine. Stoker had the suitcase, and Betty was carrying the scalps. She discarded them under a pile of rotten wood. Stoker returned outside, made a torch with dried weeds, and dashed back into the darkness of the mine. With the torch burning, the heartless killers discovered the water-filled shaft with the partial ladder and the rope draped over the edge.

Ignoring the rope, Stoker decided to hang the suitcase on the fourth rung of the ladder, just below the one where Gary Donovan had tied the rope. The outlaw fastened the suitcase handle to the fourth rung with a piece of wire he found in a dusty, discarded toolbox nearby.

Stoker and Betty backed out of the mine, using tumbleweeds to brush away their footprints from around the mine entrance. They looked the scene over, pleased with their work. Once the army heard their story and investigated this spot, the Apaches would be the scapegoats. When the investigation was over and things had cooled down, the two of them could return to the mine, grab the money, and hop a stagecoach to California.

"Now comes the hard part," Stoker said, pulling his gun. "We've got to make this look real."

While Betty clenched her teeth for the pain that was coming, Stoker fired carefully, searing a bullet along the upper part of her left arm. Betty shot him in turn, nicking his right shoulder. After tying on bandages made from her petticoats, they headed for Dragoon Springs, a walk of a little less than three miles, and on their way they rehearsed the story they would tell the army.

The lone occupant of the station was Erskine Holloway, the Butterfield agent. He was shocked to see the bloody pair come stumbling through the door. Rising at the table where he had been sitting, he swore and said, "What happened?"

Stoker assisted Betty to a couch and helped her to lie down. "Apaches," gasped Stoker. "Ambushed us over by the old Rawhide mine. Everybody else is dead."

Holloway immediately summoned the doctor from the nearby town of Dragoon Springs and wired Colonel Johnston at Fort Bowie.

The doctor had stitched up and properly bandaged the wounds when Colonel Brett Johnston, Captain Hale Wilson, and a squad of two dozen men arrived at the station. It had taken them just over an hour and a half to saddle up and ride to Dragoon Springs. Betty was lying on the couch. When she saw Hale come through the door, she went into her act, weeping and reaching for him like a lost little girl.

Hale held his wife in his arms while Stoker and Betty told the story to Colonel Johnston. The colonel was furious and swore that the Apaches would pay for this horrendous deed. Satisfied that Betty was going to be all right, Hale Wilson rode to the bloody scene at Rawhide with the colonel and the troopers.

Johnston's wrath grew hotter against the Apaches when they found the six victims sprawled around the stagecoach, each one displaying a red, meaty mass where the scalp had been cut off. He decided to bury the victims on the spot rather than haul the bodies to the fort, thinking it would be best that Elizabeth Simmons not see the mutila-

tion of her husband's body. Shallow graves were dug, and
the dead were buried, wrapped in army blankets. The
soldiers unhitched the three horses from the coach so they
could be returned to the Dragoon Springs station. A thorough search of the area failed to turn up the suitcase
containing the San Bernardino payroll. The bullet-riddled
stagecoach was then pushed into the mouth of the mine.

Colonel Brett Johnston was seething when he mounted
up and led his men back toward the station. Fury ran like
liquid fire in his veins. Not only had the Apaches massacred two soldiers and four civilians, but they had stolen a
hundred thousand dollars of United States Army funds.
He promised himself that the guilty Chiricahuas would
pay for their reckless bloodshed and that Cochise would
give the money back.

Betty Wilson was sitting up and drinking coffee with
Erskine Holloway and Red Stoker when the soldiers returned and the two officers entered the station house.
Hale Wilson sat down beside his wife. Holloway poured
coffee for Johnston and Hale.

Johnston paced back and forth in his fury, carrying his
cup with him. "I must get all the details from you that I
can," he told the two survivors. "How many Apaches were
in the war party?"

Betty and Stoker both told him there were six or seven.

"Could you identify them if you saw them again?" queried the colonel.

Betty had been waiting for him to ask this question.
Swallowing, she said, "It all happened so fast, Colonel,
but I did get a good look at a couple of them."

While Johnston carefully wrote down what she said,
Betty described the two Indians she had clearly seen at
the Apache Pass station that morning.

Holding Betty's hand, Hale exclaimed, "It's a miracle
that you two escaped alive. How in the world did you do
it?"

Stoker gave a wordy account of how he and Betty had
made their way to a rock enclosure during the shooting.
They had both been hit when the bullets were chewing
into the stagecoach, but because of all the dust and smoke

they had been able to get out undetected and hide themselves amid the rocks. When the Apaches found the suitcase full of money, they had ridden away barking like wild dogs, forgetting about the two passengers who had escaped.

Johnston agreed with Hale that the escape was indeed miraculous. Turning to Red Stoker, he said, "Will you come to the fort and help Betty identify the Indians who attacked you?"

Stoker nodded, saying, "Yes, but I can only spare a day or two, Colonel. I really must catch the next stage to Tucson."

When the soldiers and the supposed victims arrived at Fort Bowie, the story of the incident spread fast. Rayva Johnston was assigned by her father to care for Betty Wilson in the captain's quarters, while Lieutenant Gary Donovan was told to take Red Stoker—still going by the name Smith—to the unmarried officers' quarters and see that he was made comfortable.

Before Donovan left with Stoker, he heard the colonel tell Hale to assemble three hundred men at dawn and to hitch up the howitzers. They were going to ride to the Dragoons and make Cochise produce the two warriors described by Betty. When Stoker had been questioned, he had not been able to add anything to Betty's description of the two Indians, so the other four or five savages would probably never pay for their deed, the colonel said. But the two she could identify would pay with their lives.

Moments later, Red Stoker and Gary Donovan were alone in the officers' quarters, Stoker sitting on the bunk Donovan had assigned him, grimacing with pain from his bullet wound.

Through clenched teeth Stoker growled, "I hate Indians. Especially Apaches. If I had my way, we'd feed 'em all rat poison and be rid of 'em."

A plan began to form in Gary Donovan's mind, and choosing his words carefully, he said, "I hate the Apache scum, too. Especially since one of them happened to be in the right place at the right time and save the life of Colonel Johnston's adopted daughter. She and I were engaged to be married—the wedding date was even set.

But she's half Apache, and that snake that saved her life has wormed his way in, using their Apache kinship to break us up."

Stoker swore, shaking his head. Putting a cigarillo in his mouth, he fished for a match in his shirt pocket and said, "Why don't you kill the skunk?"

Donovan knew his plan was working. "It's not as easy as that," he said woefully. "He's one of Cochise's sons."

"I'd still find a way if I was you," said Stoker coldly, thumbing the match into flame.

"I think I just did." The lieutenant grinned.

Puffing smoke, the outlaw said, "How's that?"

"You can help me. I'll give you five hundred dollars if you do."

"I'm all ears."

"When you and Betty get your chance to identify the two Apaches she got a good look at, you could suddenly remember another one—Brondo. That's the skunk's name." Moving to a nearby desk, Donovan picked up a pencil and paper, saying, "I'll write a thorough description of him for you. Memorize it real good and then destroy the paper."

Stoker chuckled. "For five hundred dollars I can suddenly remember any Indian." Taking another draw on his cigarillo, he asked, "What's likely to be done with the Apaches we identify?"

Still writing, Donovan replied, "Lawmen are as scarce as hen's teeth here in Arizona. Any crime involving army personnel as victims is handled by the army. The Apaches you and Betty identify will be hanged." Donovan stood up and handed the written description of Brondo to Stoker.

The outlaw read what Donovan had written and said with a sly grin, "Yep, that dirty savage sure enough was among 'em. How could I forget a redskin that looks like that?"

The lieutenant patted him on the shoulder. "I thought you were a man I could do business with. I'll give you the five hundred in a little while. Right now I have to go and talk to the colonel."

Red Stoker lay back on the cot and blew smoke rings

toward the ceiling as Donovan disappeared through the door.

Five minutes later, Lieutenant Gary Donovan was in Colonel Brett Johnston's office, taking a seat in front of the big desk.

"What is it you wanted to see me about, Gary?" asked the colonel.

"Well, sir, I've been doing some thinking about this ambush situation, and I have a suggestion."

Nodding, Johnston smiled and said, "All right, I'm listening."

Adjusting himself to a more comfortable position on the chair, the lieutenant said, "Colonel, I am not implying that this has not crossed your mind, but we could get a lot of men killed by approaching Cochise's domain with a show of force. Even though we have the howitzers, if Cochise decided to fight, there would be a lot of army blood spilled. Sir, an idea came to me a few minutes ago that I think might prevent that."

Johnston nodded. "Proceed."

There was an evil light in Donovan's eyes. "Why not get Cochise by the nose? We both know Brondo will show up soon to see Rayva again. Why not wait until he does and then take him captive? Hold him as a hostage, and for ransom demand that the Apaches who attacked the stagecoach be turned over to you. At least make Cochise bring in the two Indians Mrs. Wilson described. All those stinking Apaches dress differently, so Cochise will know who they are. Tell him if he doesn't produce them, you'll hang his son. You'll have him by the nose. You know he'll never let us hang Brondo."

Brett Johnston frowned. Donovan's idea strongly appealed to him, especially in light of the attack on the stagecoach. But to threaten to take the life of the man who had saved Rayva from death disturbed him.

"Gary, your idea makes sense, but I have some reservations about using the young man who saved my daughter's life that way."

"I understand your concern, sir, but consider the alternative. Many lives would be lost if we used force—maybe

even Brondo's. And the Apaches didn't hesitate to kill
those passengers on the stagecoach. Wouldn't it be better
to use him to get the killers—and save all those lives, red
and white, in the process?"

The colonel tented his fingers and frowned thoughtfully
for a few moments as the lieutenant remained silent. The
brutal murders that the Apaches had committed angered
him fiercely, especially since two of his men had been
among the victims. Finally Johnston rose and said, "It's
true that the killers have to be caught and dealt with.
And," he mused, smiling, "your plan might even have the
effect of cooling the friendship between Brondo and my
daughter. I appreciate what the Apache did—saving her
life—but I don't believe she has to befriend one of a
murderous breed out of gratitude. I'll give your plan full
consideration, Gary, but I'll want to interrogate Brondo
before I make a final decision."

Donovan smiled broadly. Maybe he would win Rayva's
heart after all.

Leaving the colonel, Donovan returned to the officers'
quarters and found Red Stoker still alone. He informed
the man he knew as Smith of the plan, telling him that if
all went well, Stoker would get the opportunity to set his
eyes on Brondo and point the finger of accusation. Stoker
laughed, saying that for five hundred dollars he would
point his finger at anybody.

Brondo and his companions had ridden away from the
Apache Pass station only minutes after the stagecoach had
left that morning. They rode the desert until the sun was
touching the western horizon. Brondo continued to think
about Rayva, the love in his heart spurring him on. He
must see her again tonight.

Sending his five warriors home, he made a beeline for
Fort Bowie and pulled up at the gate as twilight settled
over the land. The sentries on duty this time opened the
gate and let him in without question, much to Brondo's
pleasure. He figured that they must have been present
when he had saved Rayva's life. As was customary, one of

the sentries ushered him to the door of the colonel's quarters.

Brondo slid off the Appaloosa's back and started toward the door, hoping that Rayva would answer his knock. But before he had stepped onto the porch, the door opened and the colonel appeared, closing the door behind him.

"Brondo to see Miss Rayva, sir," the sentry said.

"Wait right here a minute, Scully," Johnston said to the sentry. Turning his eyes on the Apache in the dim light, he grunted, "Rayva is busy right now, Brondo. She cannot see you."

Brondo was about to ask politely when he could return to see her when he suddenly found himself facing the colonel's drawn and cocked revolver. Behind the gun, Johnston's features were cold and stiff. Brondo blinked with surprise. The sentry, seeing Johnston's action, quickly brought up the muzzle of his rifle, eased back the hammer, and lined the weapon on Brondo's chest.

Brondo's rifle was still in his hand, and again to his astonishment he heard the colonel call for the soldiers who were milling around to surround and disarm him.

"Colonel, I do not understand," he said.

There was a belligerent edge to Johnston's voice as he rasped, "The stage that left Apache Pass this morning was ambushed the other side of Dragoon Springs. Apaches did it. Killed two soldiers and four civilians, and wounded two others. Stole a bundle of army payroll money, too! If you weren't in on it, you sure do know about it. And I'm telling you right now, Brondo, there's going to be the devil to pay!"

Calmly holding his composure, Brondo looked the colonel straight in the eye and said evenly, "I know nothing of any such ambush, sir. If it was Apaches, they were from another tribe. Perhaps the Mimbres or the White Mountain Apaches. They were not Chiricahuas."

Shock ran through Brondo when Johnston lashed back, "Is there a Chiricahua who wears an old Derby hat and a blue denim vest with silver studs on it?"

Brondo knew instantly that the colonel was describing his man Zenta, but before he could speak, Johnston asked hotly, "How about a flat-nosed warrior who wears his hair in a long, single pigtail? His front teeth are missing, and he wears a necklace of diamondback rattlers."

Feeling contempt rise within him, Brondo said, "Is the colonel telling me that these two men you have just described were supposed to be in on the ambush of the stagecoach today?"

"Supposed, nothing!" blared Johnston. "They have been accurately described by the two survivors!"

Brondo knew by this that someone had purposely set up Ramino and Zenta to entrap them. He could not keep the agitation from showing in his face. He said bluntly, "You have just described two Chiricahuas who ride with me. There is no way they could have been in on the ambush. They have been with me all day."

Johnston squared his jaw, and a hot flash of scorn poured out of his eyes. Through his teeth, he spoke with words that came like the lash of a whip. "Then it could be that *you* led the ambush!"

Brondo pulled his breath in harshly then said in a curt, deep monotone, "I did not lead the ambush, Colonel Johnston. Neither were Ramino and Zenta in on it!"

The colonel smiled, pleased not only to learn the names of the two Apaches but also to have sufficient excuse to adopt Donovan's plan and arrest Brondo. Looking at Captain Hale Wilson, who had been standing nearby, he barked, "Captain Wilson, lock him up in the guardhouse! Put him under double guard!"

After Brondo had been led away under heavy guard, Colonel Brett Johnston returned to the privacy of his quarters, feeling confident that Gary Donovan's plan was going to work. Sitting down in an easy chair, he sighed and laid his head back. Less than a quarter of an hour had passed when the door burst open and Rayva came in with fire in her eyes. "Father!" she blurted, staring at him in disbelief. "Hale Wilson just told me what you did to Brondo!"

Straightening up in the chair, Johnston eyed her coldly and said, "I told you his people are savages."

Struggling to check the rise of panic within her, Rayva

willed herself calm and said solemnly, "Brondo is no savage, Father. He did not lead that ambush. I have told you before, he is not a cold-blooded killer."

Johnston looked up at her blankly, saying nothing.

Wheeling, Rayva headed for the door, but before she reached it, the colonel's harsh voice reached across the room to her. "Where are you going?"

Pausing only when she had her hand on the knob of the door, she replied over her shoulder, "I am going to the guardhouse to see Brondo."

"No, you're not!" Johnston bellowed. "You stay away from that Apache! I forbid you to see him!"

"But, Father," she said in a voice that was beginning to break, "he's innocent. I must—"

"No!" he cut in. Pointing a stiff finger at her, he said, "Justice is going to be done, Rayva, and you must not interfere! I repeat, you are forbidden to see him again!"

Rayva went to her room like a puppy that had been whipped. She did not come out for the rest of the evening. All night long she tossed and turned sleeplessly on her bed, her heart in turmoil.

At dawn the next morning, Lieutenant Gary Donovan led a dozen troopers toward the Chiricahua settlement in the Dragoon Mountains. There was a deep sense of satisfaction in his heart. Brondo was in the hands of the U.S. Army, and it was Donovan's genius that had put him there. He felt confident that the colonel had recognized this. After all, look at whom he had chosen to ride to Cochise's lair and issue the ultimatum!

Donovan laughed. Cochise was over the proverbial barrel. There was no doubt that Colonel Johnston's most resourceful lieutenant would return to Fort Bowie with Ramino and Zenta in tow, and they would pay for their part in the infamous ambush. But this was nothing compared to the sweet vengeance Donovan would enjoy when Brondo stretched a rope. With that hated Apache dead, Donovan would win Rayva's heart and make her his wife.

Two dozen Apaches came out of the rocks in a fan shape

as the men in blue rode up to the entrance of the Chiricahua camp. Eyeing the soldiers suspiciously, they watched as Donovan reined in and said loudly, "I am Lieutenant Gary Donovan, U.S. Army, Fort Bowie. As representative of Colonel Brett Johnston, I am here to converse with your chief."

Cochise was called for, and moments later he appeared, tall and stately as he moved among his warriors. Other Chiricahuas were gathering, but they remained in the rocks out of sight. Halting when he reached the forefront of the fanned-out braves, Cochise set black eyes on the lieutenant and said, "You wish to speak with me?"

"Yeah, Chief," Donovan said in an insolent tone. "I am here to inform you that we are holding your son Brondo as prisoner at Fort Bowie."

Cochise had been worried over Brondo's failure to return home the night before and had been preparing a search party when the soldiers appeared. "You are holding my son for what reason?" he demanded.

"Let's just say that at this point Brondo is being held for ransom."

"Ransom? What is the ransom?"

"Two of your warriors. Zenta and Ramino."

The two Apaches named were present. They looked at each other in puzzlement and then back at Donovan.

"I do not understand," said Cochise.

Donovan waggled his head in a cocky manner. "There was a stagecoach ambushed just outside Dragoon Springs yesterday, Chief. Your bloody cutthroats were sloppy and let two people live. They have identified Ramino and Zenta as being in the war party."

"It is a lie!" Cochise snapped acridly. His face was as dark as burnt leather.

Ignoring the chief's denial, Donovan said, "Your killers also stole a hundred thousand dollars of army payroll. We want it back, and we want it right now."

Eyes widening, Cochise growled, "We do not have it!"

"We'll get it from you," stated the lieutenant. "I also demand that Ramino and Zenta be turned over to me for trial. If you refuse, Brondo will hang."

Donovan's last statement sent Cochise into a rage. Dark blood colored his features, and his narrowed eyes fixed on the lieutenant. With a wicked rasp in his voice, he snarled, "We will attack your fort to free my son! White soldiers will die!"

The lieutenant chuckled vengefully as he casually shifted positions in his saddle. "The colonel has already given orders, Chief. The minute you launch an attack, the two guards who are watching Brondo are to shoot him in the head. Go ahead. Attack. But you will kill your son when you do."

Cochise stood in silence, looking as though he were struggling for air. His eyes turned to ice, and Donovan felt the weight of the chief's venomous glare. He knew he would never see hatred plainer in a man's eyes.

Suddenly the baleful voice of the angry chief barked three sharp words in a language the soldier did not understand. Immediately the men in blue were locked in a circle of dark, malicious faces and found themselves looking into the black bores of two hundred threatening rifles.

The soldiers straightened in their saddles, their faces blanching white. They looked to Donovan for instructions, but the lieutenant seemed not the least bit flustered. Coolly, he eyed Cochise with disdain and said, "You really want to kill that son of yours, don't you? Better listen to me, Cochise. If we are not back at the fort by ten o'clock, Brondo will be put to death. If you take us captive or kill us, you will automatically kill your son."

While the Chiricahuas held the soldiers at gunpoint and Cochise pondered his predicament, Zenta and Ramino whispered a few words to each other and then stepped forward and stood beside their chief. Ramino looked at Donovan and said, "Zenta and I cannot let white soldiers kill Brondo. You said we will have a trial."

"That's right." Donovan nodded.

"On your word of honor? We will have a fair trial?"

"You have my word as an officer of the United States Army."

Ramino turned to Cochise and said, "It is simply a case of mistaken identity, Chief. Since Zenta and I know we were not part of the war party that attacked the stage-coach, we will go to the fort and clear ourselves. We will soon return, along with Brondo."

Gary Donovan smiled to himself. This whole thing was going to work out exactly as he had planned. Betty Wilson's testimony would hang these two worthless Apaches, and Red Smith's testimony would doubtless put Brondo's neck in the noose. Between Donovan and the colonel, they would figure out a way to get the payroll money back.

Cochise realized that he had no choice but to allow his two warriors to go. Brondo's life depended on it. He stood with mixed emotions as he watched Ramino and Zenta ride away with the soldiers. There was a ray of hope that Brondo and his two friends would return unharmed and the episode would be over. But there was also suspicion lurking in the back of his mind, and feelings of doubt in his heart.

Chapter Twelve

Rayva Johnston bit down hard on her lower lip, fighting tears, as she washed the breakfast dishes. She had not touched a bite, but her father had filled himself and gone to his office. The heavy-hearted young woman was feeling the effects of her sleepless night. She thought of Gary Donovan and the dozen men whom she had seen leave the fort an hour before dawn, and she shuddered when she thought of the plans she had heard them discussing. There was going to be real trouble from the Apaches.

Drying her hands and removing the apron that she wore, Rayva settled an argument she was having with herself. It would go against her grain to defy her father, but the love in her heart for Brondo was too strong. She had to see him.

The two guards who stood just outside the guardhouse door smiled as they saw the raven-haired young woman approach. Rayva was sure neither was aware that the colonel had forbidden her to see their Apache prisoner.

"Good morning, gentlemen!" Rayva said cheerfully. "I have come to see Brondo. May I go in, please?"

The guards looked at each other, and then one of them said, "Of course, ma'am. It would be best if you only stayed ten or fifteen minutes, though."

"That will be fine," she assured him.

The door was held open for her, and after Rayva stepped through into the dim interior, the door closed behind her.

There were only two small windows in the guardhouse, with tiny streamers of sunshine letting in a little light. There were three cells, with a narrow corridor running between the bars and the outside wall. The first two cells were unoccupied. Brondo was in the third.

When Rayva heard Brondo's deep voice speak her name, she dashed down the corridor. His muscular arms were extended through the bars of his cell, reaching for her.

"Oh, Brondo!" she cried as she pressed herself to the bars and he folded his arms around her.

Looking into her dark, tearful eyes, he said, "Thank you for coming."

Rayva tilted her face toward his, and they kissed tenderly through the bars. Clinging to his arms, she said, "I had to disobey my father to come here, but I could not help it. Oh, Brondo, I love you!"

"And I love you, my beautiful Rayva," he breathed.

They kissed again, and then she said in a sorrowful tone, "I know you were not a part of the ambush, but I am afraid my father is going to hang you."

"Ramino and Zenta were not a part of it either," he said. "It is my guess that the two survivors must have seen Ramino and Zenta at the relay station yesterday morning, and for some reason they want to make the army believe my two men were part of the war party."

"But why?" she asked, releasing a hand from his arm to wipe away a tear.

"I lay awake all night thinking about it," he replied. "I have begun to wonder if there really was an ambush."

"What do you mean?"

"Rayva, when Apaches attack stagecoaches or wagon trains, they do not leave survivors."

"Then . . . what do you think happened? I tended to Betty Wilson's wound myself. She was shot in the arm. The man who survived with her was shot, too, and Captain Wilson told me that he helped bury the others. They had been scalped, and the stagecoach was riddled with bullets. Would the Hopis or the Yaquis have done it?"

"The Hopis and the Yaquis have no love for the whites," commented Brondo, "but neither tribe is hostile. I have never known them to launch an offensive against white men. And they are not scalpers, either."

"Well, then, who could have done it, Brondo?"

Leveling his eyes on hers, he said, "The two survivors."

Rayva's mouth fell open, followed by a tight intake of breath. "But why? How—"

"Money," he answered flatly. "A hundred thousand dollars of it. White people will do evil things for money, Rayva. The two survivors—they were not shot very bad, were they?"

"Only superficial wounds," she admitted. Twisting her face, she said, "I don't know the man at all, but it's hard to picture Betty Wilson as a killer. I've never cared much for her, but she never struck me as being capable of . . . of that."

"Rayva, if I could examine the stagecoach and the area where this ambush happened, I might find some clue to the truth."

"Then it must be done," Rayva replied instantly. "Tell me what I can do to help get you out of here."

Shaking his head, the muscular Apache said, "I do not want you involved."

"I am already involved," protested Rayva. "I am in love with you . . . and I'm afraid Father will hang you if you don't clear yourself."

Tightening his grip on her, Brondo said, "I cannot cause a problem between you and your father."

"There won't be a problem once you prove you are innocent," she said, tears surfacing again. "You saved my life once, Brondo. Now I must save yours. Gary Donovan is out at the Dragoons right now, issuing Cochise an ultimatum. I heard him and his men talking as they rode out before dawn this morning. They're telling your father he must turn Zenta and Ramino over to the army for trial or . . . or you will hang."

Brondo's bronzed forehead furrowed with deep lines. "When will the trial be held?"

"I would think just as soon as they are brought in. If they are convicted, they'll hang at sunrise." Fear filled her eyes. "Oh, Brondo," she sniffled, "if your father refuses to

give them Zenta and Ramino, my father will hang you! I
can't let that happen!"

"He would not hang me until sunrise, right?"

"That's the customary time."

"Then I must get out of here before sunrise. Even if my
father gives them Ramino and Zenta, I must prove them
innocent before sunrise."

A determined light glinted in Rayva's obsidian eyes.
"I'll return after dark tonight," she said doggedly. "Some-
how I will overpower the guards and set you free. If
Ramino and Zenta are in here, they can go with you.
You've got to clear yourselves of this charge."

"No, Rayva," Brondo argued. "I will figure a way by
myself. I cannot have you involved."

She kissed him quickly, saying she loved him, and
hurried to the door before he could say any more. She
rapped on it and was let out.

His face pressed to the bars, Brondo stared after her.
Love for Rayva Johnston flowed through him like a soft,
warm river. She was vibrant and brave, and her presence
stirred all his masculine senses. She had given his life new
meaning, and because of this, whatever the risk or the
cost, he had to live. He had to have her for his mate.

It was getting on toward noon when Lieutenant Gary
Donovan and his men filed into Fort Bowie with their
prisoners. Court was set up in the mess hall, which soon
began to fill with blue-uniformed men.

Brondo was taken from his cell and seated in the mess
hall between the two guards who had stood outside the
guardhouse. Rayva was sitting alone a few feet away. She
looked at Brondo with soft, loving eyes and smiled. He
smiled back. At that moment Gary Donovan came in and
sat down beside Rayva, and she gave him an icy stare.

Ramino and Zenta were seated up front, flanked by two
guards. Also at the front, but on the opposite side of the
room, were Red Stoker and Betty Wilson, her husband at
her side. Glancing at the two Indians, Betty saw that they

were dressed the same as they had been when she had seen them at the stage station the morning before.

Red Stoker let his eyes roam the room until he found the man who fit Donovan's description. There was no mistaking Brondo; he fit Donovan's description perfectly.

Arriving last, Colonel Brett Johnston made an impressive entrance in the packed mess hall. He seated himself at a small table in the front and declared the court in session. Then he made a brief but thorough explanation of what the trial was about, describing the ambush that had taken place at the old Rawhide mining camp. He told of the survivors' descriptions of the two Apaches in the war party that had ambushed them.

Red Stoker and Betty Wilson were each sworn in, and when that was done, the colonel said, "Mrs. Wilson, do you see the two men in this room whom you described to me yesterday as having been in the war party that ambushed the stagecoach you were riding?"

"Yes, sir, I do," answered the blond woman.

"Would you point them out, please?"

With face muscles firm and eyes steady, Betty Wilson pointed a finger at Ramino and Zenta. "Those two right there," she said evenly.

Brondo felt the temperature of his blood begin to rise. There was no question in his mind that the couple wearing the bandages had staged the whole thing. They had murdered and scalped their unsuspecting victims, stashed the money in some safe place, and then shot themselves to make their story convincing.

"How about you, Mr. Smith?" asked Johnston. "Have you seen these two men before?"

"Yes, sir, your honor," lied the outlaw. "Them two were definitely with the savages that attacked us yesterday."

Brondo's face was livid.

"And what's more, your honor," Stoker said, "I just spotted another one."

"Another what?" queried the colonel.

"Another one of the killers that ambushed our stage."

The colonel arched his eyebrows. "Oh? Would you point him out, please?"

"Sure," said Stoker, pointing an accusing finger at Brondo. "That's him, right there!"

Rayva's jaw slacked, and Brondo stiffened. A rumble went through the roomful of men in blue. They knew that Brondo was the brave Apache who had saved the life of the colonel's daughter.

Betty Wilson did not know of the pact Red Stoker had with Gary Donovan, but when the colonel asked her if she remembered the muscular Apache known as Brondo being in the war party, she answered in the affirmative.

Anger surfaced within Brondo, and he leaped to his feet and said, "Colonel Johnston, these people are lying! Ramino and Zenta were with me all day yesterday, along with three other men. We were nowhere near Dragoon Springs!"

"We have your word against the word of these responsible citizens, Brondo," Johnston was saying. "Why would they have any reason to pick you out and lie about you?"

Betty spoke up, "Colonel, I just remembered something."

"Yes, ma'am?"

"There was a group of Apaches at the Apache Pass station when I boarded the stage yesterday morning. My husband saw them, too. I remember telling Hale my fear that they'd follow the stage and attack us. Didn't I, darling?"

"Captain Wilson," said Johnston, "you are not under oath, but I will ask you if it happened as your wife has just stated."

Nodding, Wilson said, "Yes, sir, it did. She did express that fear to me."

"Did you get a look at any of them?"

"Do you mean, sir, could I identify any of them?"

"Yes."

"No, sir. I didn't look that closely at them."

Swinging his hard gaze on Brondo, Johnston said, "I am going to ask you something, son of Cochise, and I want a truthful answer. Was that your group of warriors at Apache Springs?"

Brondo knew this line of questioning was going to condemn him and his two companions; the colonel was going to conclude that it was Brondo's group who had attacked the stage. He had no choice but to tell the truth. Still on his feet, he nodded and answered, "Yes, Colonel. It was my group. I was there, along with three other men and these two over here."

Ramino and Zenta knew that this would seal their doom. Their faces turned to stone.

Red Stoker, pleased by Betty's quick thinking, threw a furtive glance at Gary Donovan. Brondo had just hung himself and his friends.

"I know how this looks, Colonel," said Brondo, "but I tell you, we did not ambush the stage."

A grimace of disbelief curved Johnston's mouth. "You were at the Apache Pass station, but it never occurred to you to attack the stage, eh?"

"No, sir," replied Brondo.

"It didn't cross your mind?"

"No, it did not."

Squinting hard at the young Apache, the colonel asked, "Brondo, just what were you and your warriors doing at the station?"

Fright showed in Brondo's eyes. It was not in him to lie; he had been raised always to be truthful, believing that the truth can never truly harm you. Taking a deep breath, he said, "My father, Cochise, sent us there to make the whites nervous."

Johnston smiled wickedly, easing back in his chair. "Oh, is that so? And you expect me to believe that there was no more to it than that?"

"It is the truth, sir," came Brondo's reply.

"Well, I don't believe it!" snapped Johnston. "And nobody with a brain in his head would believe it, either! Sit down, Brondo."

Two strong hands touched Brondo's shoulders, and he reluctantly settled back on his chair.

Running his gaze over the crowd, Johnston said, "Since there is no jury in this trial, the verdict is up to me. Proper testimony has been given to convince me of the guilt of these Apaches. There is no question in my mind that these three and three others attacked the Butterfield stage yesterday, massacring six innocent people. They also stole a hundred thousand dollars of army funds, which we are going to retrieve, and we will bring the other three killers to justice. In the meantime I sentence Brondo, Ramino, and Zenta to hang by the neck until dead. The execution will take place at sunrise tomorrow. Court is adjourned."

Brondo was seething inside. Unless he could escape to produce evidence that the man and woman were lying, there was no way to clear himself and his friends. Not wanting to involve Rayva, he decided to make an escape attempt immediately. It was a long shot, but what did he have to lose?

"Let's go, Brondo," said one of his guards.

Rising, the Apache unleashed a sledgehammer blow to the guard, sending him reeling into a cluster of men getting in line to file out of the building. With the quickness of a cat, Brondo snatched the other guard's revolver, flung him to the floor, and jammed the muzzle into his mouth.

Brondo heard a woman scream. He glanced up to see that Rayva had risen, shock registering on her face. Colonel Johnston was standing behind the desk, frozen to the spot. No one in the building moved.

Thumbing back the hammer, Brondo shouted, "Anyone comes near me, this man dies! I do not want to kill him, but I must leave these premises to produce evidence that those two people are lying. This guard and I are going to leave the fort. The gun will stay in his mouth until we are a safe distance away."

Rayva's hand was covering her mouth, and fear filled her eyes.

Looking down at the guard, Brondo said, "I will do you no harm, soldier, if your men do not try to interfere. Now get up. We are leaving."

Suddenly Gary Donovan's voice came like a battering ram across the room. "You're not going anywhere, Brondo!"

Brondo turned to see Donovan gripping Zenta by the neck and head. There was a devilish look in the lieutenant's eyes.

"Take the gun out of his mouth, Brondo," Donovan

rasped, "or so help me, I'll blow your friend's brains all over Arizona!"

Despair gripped the young Apache. He could do nothing but obey. Removing the gun from the guard's mouth, he stood up and eased the hammer down. Immediately, he was surrounded by blue uniforms.

Strong hands grabbed his arms as he looked through the crowd at Rayva. Her eyes filled with tears as she looked at him. As he was led away he saw her raise a gloved hand and wave at him uncertainly, as if she did not know what to do. Brondo smiled warmly at her and saw her face light up, and his heart was renewed.

The guards took Brondo to his cell in the guardhouse, and as a precaution the colonel had Ramino and Zenta incarcerated in separate places in the compound. Ramino was chained in the toolshed, Zenta in the harness and saddle shack. Colonel Johnston assigned Hale Wilson to secure them.

While Hale was attending to the Indians, his wife and Red Stoker stood casually talking in front of the mess hall as the crowd dispersed. When no one was looking, they stepped inside. They didn't want to be overheard, and at the moment the building was empty.

Red took her in his arms and kissed her. Then he said, "Honey, we've got it made! There's another stagecoach coming through in the morning. I'll board it and ride to Dragoon Springs. Then I'll get my hands on a horse and ride to the mine, take the money, and ride to the town of Willcox. Can you figure out a way to get to Willcox without raising suspicions?"

Smiling widely, she said, "It'll be a cinch. There's another sewing bee in Bowie in three days. I'll attend at first—to make everything look good—then after the women get to gabbing, I'll excuse myself, saying I'm going to do a little shopping. I'll hire a buggy to take me to Willcox and meet you wherever you say, and we'll pull a disappearing act."

"Wonderful!" he exclaimed. "Meet me at the Red Rose Saloon. I'll have a horse for you. We'll ride to Tucson and catch a stage from there to California."

"It's a deal," said Betty, pulling him to her.

As they were kissing, Trooper Gerald Holmes entered the back door of the mess hall. He was on kitchen duty and was coming in to get things rolling for the noon meal. When he saw Red and Betty kissing, he backed out of the building quietly, unnoticed by them.

Colonel Brett Johnston had just sat down at his desk when the office door came open. He looked up to see his adopted daughter standing there, tears in her eyes.

Putting his palms up, he said, "Don't say it, Rayva. You're going to try to tell me Brondo is innocent, but you're wasting your breath. He's as guilty as sin, and you know it."

"I don't know it, Father," she retorted, "and neither do you! You heard Brondo say that he can get evidence to prove that Smith and that . . . that woman are lying. Why don't you go ask him what evidence he is talking about and give him a chance to explain it to you?"

Brett Johnston was seething with anger, and his face took on a sallow, wicked expression. "How can you go on defending that bloodthirsty savage?" he demanded scornfully. "You should have listened to me in the first place. I tried to cut him off the day he kept you from going over the cliff, but you had to be so nice to him! I was right all along. He's a heartless killer just like his father! He's going to hang for what he did, Rayva. And when he's dead, you can give your attention to Gary again—as you should have been doing in the first place!"

Rayva stood staring at him for several seconds. Then, without another word, she turned and left the office.

Night came, and Rayva, full of determination to see Brondo, waited for the soldiers in the fort to bed down. Making sure her father was asleep in his room, she took one of his revolvers and climbed out her bedroom window. Stealthily she slipped through the shadows and moved up to the guardhouse.

Just as she ducked behind a corner of the building, she saw one of the two guards step inside with a lantern in his hand and close the door. Taking advantage of the moment, she hastened along the wall, seeing by the dim light that the remaining guard was facing the other way. Gripping the barrel of the Colt .45 in her hand, she brought the butt down violently on the guard's head, and he collapsed in a heap. At that instant she heard the footsteps of the guard inside, coming toward the door. Quickly she turned the gun in her hands and eared back the hammer. When the door came open, she thrust the muzzle at the guard, saying in a hoarse whisper, "Stop right there, Harry!"

Trooper Harry Neal could not believe what was happening. He would never have thought Rayva capable of putting a gun on someone. The wild look in her eyes convinced him to obey, and holding the lantern in one hand and his rifle in the other, he said, "Miss Rayva, I don't know what you've got in mind, but you'd be much better off if you'd forget it."

Aiming the muzzle between his eyes, she said, "No lectures, Harry. Just back inside." When Neal obeyed, Rayva followed him in and pushed the door shut with her foot.

Brondo was on his feet, standing with his hands on the bars, when they entered. He was stunned to see Rayva holding a gun on the guard, and he feared for her safety. Yet he knew it was too late to tell her to turn back.

He watched her as she tensely told Harry Neal to set the lantern down and release Brondo from his cell. It took only a moment for Neal to comply, and Brondo then stepped out of the cell, wondering if Rayva wanted him to take over for her. But at that moment she asked him to go out and drag the other guard inside while she backed Neal into Brondo's cell. Brondo brought the unconscious guard in and bound him and Neal, all the while thinking of what to do about Ramino and Zenta. He knew it was too risky to try to find them and set them free now, so as he was tying up Harry Neal, he said to the trooper, "I want you to give a message to Colonel Johnston."

Neal eyed the muzzle of Rayva's gun as she held it trained on him and said to Brondo, "What is it?"

"Tell him I am bringing evidence that will prove Red

Smith and Betty Wilson are lying about the ambush. I told him the truth when I said none of us had anything to do with it. Tell him he must not hang Ramino and Zenta. He must hold off until Rayva and I return. Do you understand?"

"Yes," Neal said, nodding. "I'll get the message to the colonel."

Neal and the unconscious guard were gagged quickly, and then Brondo and the woman he loved moved through the shadows to the corral. After quietly bridling his Appaloosa and leading it and a big bay gelding out of the enclosure, Brondo and Rayva swung onto their mounts and rode across the night-shaded desert toward Rawhide.

Through the gray gloom of early dawn, Brondo and Rayva skirted the town of Dragoon Springs and headed in a straight line for the abandoned mining camp.

The horizon was filling with orange shafts of sunlight as they hauled up and dismounted near the dark mouth of the mine. Brondo took note of the stagecoach sitting just inside the wide opening. Then he looked toward the six mounds of earth nearby.

"What are you looking for?" Rayva asked.

Brondo slid from the Appaloosa's back and then helped Rayva down. As he lowered her to the earth, he looked into her deep, expressive eyes and said, "I am looking for a way to live my life out with you."

"Oh, Brondo," she breathed.

He pulled her close, and as she tilted her face toward his, their heartbeats blended simultaneously with their lips.

"To answer your question," he said, smiling, "I want to examine the stagecoach, but first I want to look around for anything unusual."

Rayva walked beside him as he made a wide circle, studying the ground. There were a myriad of hoofprints, indicating that many horses had been on the spot at one time. Brondo followed the prints to the edge of the immediate area and then began walking in the direction of Dragoon Springs. He stopped some fifty yards out, with

Rayva flanking him, and broadly scanning the area, he said, "Just as I thought."

"What?" Rayva asked.

Brondo pointed out that the stagecoach would not have been able to make a sudden stop if Apaches had come riding up in an ambush. It would have had to roll to a stop. But there were no hoofprints running alongside the wheelmarks of the coach. As they walked back toward the old mining camp, Rayva asked, "Why didn't my father and the other soldiers notice this?"

Brondo chuckled dryly. "They were not looking for any such evidence. They believed Mrs. Wilson and Red Smith about the Apache ambush. This is also why they did not wonder why no Indian pony hoofmarks were here, even where all the killing took place. Every hoofmark is that of a shod horse. Apaches do not shoe their horses, and your father surely knows this. The army horses left their prints, but there are no others."

"My father's hatred for the Apaches has clouded his mind," Rayva said, shaking her head. "We must get him out here and show this to him before a rain destroys the evidence."

"We may not need it," Brondo commented quietly. "What we find when we examine the stagecoach may be enough."

Rayva watched as he walked into the mouth of the mine, took hold of the tongue of the coach, and rolled it out into the sunlight. "Oh, my!" she exclaimed. "Look at all the bullet holes!"

Brondo dropped the tongue and walked around the bullet-riddled vehicle. Shaking his head in disbelief, he said, "Your father and his men are not thinking at all, Rayva. Come. Walk all the way around the coach and tell me what is wrong with what you see."

Rayva made the circle, letting her dark eyes dart from bullet hole to bullet hole.

"Well?" said Brondo.

The beautiful half-breed smiled firmly and said, "The bullets have entered the stagecoach from every direction.

If this was done while the Apaches were attacking the stage, they were shooting through it at each other."

"Yes!" said the Apache, smiling proudly. "You are right."

Brondo went to the right side of the coach, stepped up on the wheel, and looked into the driver's box. He noted the large amount of blood that had pooled on the seat and the floor, and then he carefully examined the blood-splattered bullet holes in the back of the seat on the shotgunner's side. Stepping down, he opened the coach door, climbed inside, and calling Rayva to him, showed her two bullet holes in the front part of the roof, indicating that the shotgunner had been killed by someone shooting from the back seat inside the coach.

Rayva nodded, backed out of the coach, and said, "When Father gets a look at this, he'll be convinced that Betty and Smith are lying. It is hard to believe that she could have done this awful thing . . . but the evidence is there."

"I think I can get more proof," Brondo said, heading for the six graves.

Rayva watched as he clawed through the fresh dirt of a grave, exhuming the blanket-wrapped body. It happened to be that of Lieutenant Don Simmons. Rayva's stomach gave her a bit of trouble, but she followed Brondo's finger as he pointed out that Simmons had been shot in the chest from a level angle, not from ambushers outside the vehicle. There were also telltale powder burns on his shirt. He had been shot from no more than four feet away. When the bullet was dug out, Brondo said, he was sure it would be from a revolver. The colonel surely knew that Apaches fought with rifles, not revolvers.

Brondo deposited Simmons's body in the stagecoach and then dug through the remaining graves until he found the body of the shotgunner. As he had expected, he found that the young man had been shot in the back at an angle that indicated that the bullet could only have come from inside the passenger compartment. After placing the shotgunner's body inside the coach, Brondo told Rayva that they would pull the coach to Fort Bowie with their two horses, using some rope he had spotted in the box.

With the truth figured out, the handsome Apache commented to Rayva that Smith and Betty must have hidden the payroll money nearby, intending to come back and get it later. Rayva's eyes swung to the mouth of the mine.

"Our minds think as one. That is just what I was thinking." He grinned.

Remembering that he had felt some matches in Don Simmons's shirt pocket while examining his wound, Brondo fetched them and pulled dry weeds from near the mouth of the mine. Forming a torch with the weeds, he set it afire and started into the dark mine with Rayva on his heels. They had taken only a few steps when Brondo spotted a pile of wood that had been recently disturbed. Moving to it, he pushed the top pieces aside, exposing six bloody scalps.

Rayva made a gagging sound, covering her mouth.

"More evidence," Brondo said levelly. "Your father knows that Apaches do not hide the scalps they take. They display them proudly by wearing them on their waists and attaching them to their spears and rifles. We will take the scalps with us."

Looking down at his feet, Brondo studied the many fresh footprints leading into the mine. He squatted when among them he noticed the prints of a woman's shoes. Rising quickly, he hastened deeper into the mine, knowing exactly where to look.

Rayva took another look at the ghastly scalps and then darted after Brondo. He was leaning over the edge of the water-filled shaft as she drew alongside him.

"This is the shaft where Donovan and his men left me," he said hollowly. "And I see that Smith and Betty Wilson also found it. Hold the torch for me. The payroll is right here."

Rayva held the torch and leaned over his shoulder. Her eyes fell on the suitcase, wired to the fourth rung of the dilapidated old ladder. Within seconds, Brondo had loosened it, brought it up, and laid it on the soft earth at the lip of the dark hole. Opening the suitcase, he pulled out the two canvas bags and looked up at Rayva. Shaking them, he said, "This is what Smith and the woman killed for!"

At that moment one of the bags bumped solidly against the suitcase, and the lid slammed shut, jarring the suitcase. It toppled over the edge of the shaft, dropping into the dark water below.

Not concerned with the floating suitcase, Brondo led Rayva out of the mine. He tied the stagecoach behind the two horses, and with the money, the scalps, and the two corpses in the battered coach, he and Rayva headed slowly toward the fort, using a shortcut that avoided the road used by the Butterfield stages.

Lieutenant Gary Donovan lay on his bunk, unable to sleep. His triumph over Brondo had been sweet . . . so sweet he lay awake to savor it. He was picturing the Apache with his neck in a noose when he heard a strange sound coming from outside the building. Listening hard, he heard it again. Leaping out of bed, he slipped into his trousers, pulled on his boots, and dashed outside. Then he heard the sound again. Someone was calling for help from inside the guardhouse.

It was two hours before dawn and still quite dark, but Donovan ran toward the building as fast as he could. Just as he reached it, a sentry from the wall came dashing up. Peering at each other in the dark, they stopped.

"Lieutenant Donovan, is that you?" asked the sentry.

"Yes," responded Donovan.

"You heard it, too, huh?"

"Yes. It's coming from inside the guardhouse. I don't see the guards anywhere."

The cry for help came again, and the two soldiers dashed inside the guardhouse to find the two troopers tied up in the cell that had been occupied by Brondo. Neal had worked his gag loose and was calling out for help. The other trooper was still unconscious.

"I'll take care of them," Donovan told the sentry. "You get back to your post."

The sentry obeyed, and Gary Donovan knelt down and began to untie Neal. Donovan swore as Neal told him of

Brondo's escape and how Rayva had knocked out the other man and drawn a gun on himself.

"Lieutenant," said Neal, "Brondo left a message for me to give to the colonel. I must talk to him right away."

"What's the message?" asked Donovan, having trouble with one of the knots Brondo had tied.

"The Apache said that I should tell the colonel that he is going to produce evidence that Smith and Betty Wilson lied in court—evidence that will clear Ramino, Zenta, and Brondo in the ambush. He said the colonel shouldn't hang Ramino and Zenta. They're innocent, and he'll prove it when he returns."

"Tell you what," said Donovan, thinking fast, "I have to go wake the colonel and tell him about Brondo's escape. I'll give him the message for you."

Gary Donovan left the guardhouse as Neal was untying the other guard, who was coming around. A few minutes later he was standing before a sleepy-eyed Brett Johnston, telling him that Brondo had escaped with Rayva's help and that the two of them were gone.

Johnston swore vehemently. "That heathen has turned Rayva into a savage just like himself!"

Donovan purposely withheld Brondo's message from the colonel, but taking advantage of Johnston's state of fury, he said, "Colonel, you know Brondo is going to come with Cochise and attempt to rescue those other two Apaches. Why don't we drag them out and hang them right now? Let's teach Cochise and the rest of his pack that they can't trifle with the U.S. Army!"

"Yes, you're right," Johnston said, but then he paused, looking thoughtful. "I'm not so sure about that," he continued. "After all, Rayva is with that Apache. If we hang his friends, it might put her in danger."

"She is in no danger," Donovan pointed out. "She is half Apache, isn't she? And Brondo, as vile as he is, wouldn't let any harm come to her. She would be in more danger if the Apaches got here and found out those two Indians are still alive. Then they might decide to use her as a hostage, despite Brondo's objections. With the Indians already hanged, Brondo will see to it that no harm befalls Rayva."

Donovan gave the words a moment to sink in and then went on, "If I may say so, Colonel, the real issue here is whether the United States Army will be bullied about by a bunch of savages. If we do anything to give the impression that we are backing down, the Apaches will think they can use Rayva to get whatever they want. That would put her in even more danger."

Johnston nodded slowly. "Yes, I believe you are right. I can't let my personal situation cloud my actions." He glanced at his watch. "It is almost dawn, anyway, and we have a court-appointed sentence to carry out. Have the heathens brought out while I get dressed. I'll meet you at the gallows."

Soon the entire fort was awake. The word had spread about Rayva Johnston having freed Brondo and then run off with him. Harry Neal had taken the other guard to the post physician for examination of the knot Rayva had put on his head, and then Neal made his way to the gallows, which stood behind the stable and corral. Several men were carrying lanterns. When Neal saw Ramino and Zenta being dragged up the gallows steps, Neal figured Colonel Johnston had not believed Brondo's message and had decided to ignore it.

An hour later the men in the fort returned to their beds. Alone, Lieutenant Gary Donovan, an evil grin on his face, stood beside the gallows as the gray dawn came with a slight breeze. The limp bodies of Ramino and Zenta hung silhouetted against the brightening sky, swaying gently.

Chapter Thirteen

The next morning Betty Wilson kissed her husband as he left their quarters for the day's duties. Then she congratulated herself on the success of her scheme. When she and Stoker got to California, she would arrange a little accident for him, and the whole hundred thousand would be hers.

Ten minutes after Hale had left, Betty was primping in front of a bedroom mirror when she heard the front door slam. Heavy footsteps thundered across the outer room, and suddenly the tall, broad-shouldered captain filled the bedroom doorway. Not bothering to turn around, Betty looked at him in the mirror. His face was flushed with fury. The blaze in his eyes pulled her head around, and she felt the power of his hostility.

"You slut!" his angry voice shot across the room.

Betty's jaw slacked. Blinking her eyes in feigned amazement, she said, "Hale, darling, what are you so angry about?"

"Don't call me *darling*!" he hissed through clenched teeth. "Gerald Holmes just told me he saw you kissing Red Smith in the mess hall after the trial yesterday!"

Stunned, Betty stammered, "Hale, I . . . I . . ."

"Don't bother denying it, slut!" he railed. "I can see you're never going to change. Pack up and get out!"

Volcanic heat ignited in Betty's blood. She did not have to listen to the high and mighty Captain Hale Wilson call her names—she didn't need him anymore. A hundred thousand dollars would soon be hers. Suddenly her features lined heavily with rage, and the skin around her full, red lips grooved with contempt. With a wicked sneer, she spat out, "Who needs you? I hate your ever-livin' guts, Hale Wilson!"

Moving across the room to stare him square in the face, she spewed, "You want to know the truth, big man? I've wanted to throw up every time you've kissed me! I've been living for the day when you would ride out of this stinking fort and stop an Apache bullet! So what do you think of that?"

"Pack up and get out," Hale said thinly. His voice was cold, like a gust of wind off a frozen lake.

Hands on hips, Betty said, "The stage already left. I'll have to wait until the next stage comes through, day after tomorrow."

"Fine," he rasped. "Be on it." With that he wheeled, stomped through their quarters, charged out the door, and slammed it violently.

Her hands still on her hips, the virulent blond woman laughed aloud. This would work out fine. She could take the stage to Dragoon Springs and then hire a buggy to take her to Willcox, where Red Stoker and the money would be waiting.

Earlier that morning, Red Stoker had bid the colonel good-bye, walked to the Butterfield station, and boarded the stagecoach.

When the uneventful trip was over, he walked the few short miles from Dragoon Springs to the old Rawhide mine. While moving briskly across the cactus-strewn desert, he made a decision: Hale Wilson could keep his wife. Stoker would take the hundred thousand dollars all for himself. He would pull the money out of the shaft, steal a horse from a nearby ranch, and hightail it for Los Angeles. "After all," he said to himself, "when you've got money, beautiful women are a dime a dozen."

He entered the mouth of the mine, so intent on getting his hands on the money that he did not notice that the stagecoach was gone. Lighting matches, he made his way back toward the shaft.

The match in his hand was going out just as he reached the black hole. Lighting a fresh one, he leaned over the edge to peer down, and an icy blade stabbed his heart when he did not see the suitcase, which he had left attached to the ladder. He uttered several profane words, but then the light from the match revealed the suitcase below, floating on the dark water.

With a sigh of relief, he said, "Guess the wire was too old and brittle to hold it."

Seeing that there was still a rope hanging over the edge of the shaft, he lit another match, and in its light he ran his eye up and down the rope, gauging it to be long enough to lower him to where he could retrieve the suitcase. He would have to do it in the dark, but for a man as resourceful as himself, he figured, that posed no problem. To be safe, he tested the knot where the rope was tied to the third rung of the ladder and found it secure.

Shaking out the burning match, he took hold of the rope, eased his body over the edge, and began his descent into the pitch-black shaft. He could hear the water below slapping the wall. As he worked his way downward, the frayed ends of the rope touched his hands, but since his fingers did not grip the spot where Lieutenant Gary Donovan had sawed through it with a knife—and since he was so eager to get the money—the irregularity in the rope failed to register in his mind. There were only a few strands left.

Stoker was a heavier man than Brondo, and when his weight tugged against the few remaining threads of hemp, they began to come apart. Reaching the end of the rope, he braced his feet against the wall of the shaft and, hanging on to the rope with one hand, reached down, groping toward the water in the darkness. The lapping of the water and the scuffling sound of his boots against the wall masked the sound of the snapping strands of rope above him.

Swearing profusely, he searched for the handle of the suitcase. When his fingers closed around it, he laughed wildly, yelling out, "Sorry, Betty! You know how it is with money! The Good Book says that the love of it is the root of all evil. When you get to Willcox and find old Red gone, you'll know he was just too evil!"

Suddenly Stoker felt the rope jerk as the last strands began to give way. Instinctively he stiffened, attempting to brace his feet against one side of the shaft and his back against the other. For a moment he was suspended there, but then he began to slide helplessly downward. "No!" he cried. *"No!"*

Within seconds the outlaw was in the cold, black water, thrashing, screaming, and clawing at the wall of the shaft. Gagging between screams, he took water into his lungs. The struggle went on for several minutes. Knowing he was going to die, Stoker clutched the suitcase to his chest. His body gave one last spasm as he sank beneath the surface. Then all was still.

At the Apache camp in the Dragoons, Cochise paced back and forth in front of his lodge as Geronimo and a horde of worried warriors stood nearby. Cochise, his face set in deep lines, paused for a moment and said, "Geronimo, if Brondo, Zenta, and Ramino are not back by noon, the entire Chiricahua force will mount up. We will go to the fort after them!"

Geronimo smiled, nodding. That was *his* way of handling the white man—force.

At high noon the guard on duty at the gate of Fort Bowie squinted his eyes against the sun's glare and studied the black dot that was moving toward him on the desert. Holding his gaze on it, he watched it come closer until it resolved itself into an Appaloosa and an army bay pulling a stagecoach.

Turning, the guard shouted, "Hey! Somebody get the colonel!"

A crowd led by Colonel Brett Johnston gathered at the gate as the bullet-riddled stagecoach was towed inside the fort. The tail end of the coach passed through, and the gate was quickly closed. As the colonel approached his daughter and the Apache, Brondo took note of the eight howitzers placed on platforms around the perimeter of the stockade walls. The fort was ready for Cochise.

Hale Wilson stood beside Johnston, who glared at his daughter and then at Brondo. "What is this all about?" he demanded.

"This is the evidence I told you about in my message, Colonel," said the Apache, sliding down from his horse..

Looking at Brondo's back while the Indian helped Rayva from her horse, Johnston said, "What message?"

Turning around as Rayva's feet touched the ground, Brondo replied, "The message I gave the guard."

"Harry Neal," spoke up Rayva, in an attempt to clarify the matter.

Blinking and shaking his head, the colonel said, "I received no message from Neal."

"Certainly you have found the two guards by now!" exclaimed Rayva.

"Of course," snapped Johnston. "You two hadn't been gone more than a few hours when Neal awakened the place. But he gave me no message."

"He assured me that he would," said Brondo, perturbed. "He was to tell you that I would produce evidence that Red Smith and Betty Wilson were lying about the ambush. I told you yesterday in the mess hall that I would prove the innocence of my friends and myself by producing such evidence. That is why I put the gun in the soldier's mouth and tried to escape." Pointing at the battered coach, he added, "*Here* is the evidence."

Colonel Brett Johnston cast a worried look at Captain Hale Wilson and said, "Show me what you mean."

Carefully and methodically, Brondo showed the colonel and the captain the same evidence of the couple's guilt that he had presented to Rayva. The bullets having entered the stagecoach from every direction, the obvious shooting of the shotgunner from inside the coach, the collection of scalps, and the angle of the bullet in Lieutenant Don Simmons's chest, along with powder burns on his shirt. Together it all served to prove that there had been no Apache ambush of the stagecoach.

While the colonel and the crowd of onlookers stood in stunned amazement, Brondo said, "I am sure, Colonel, that you know Apaches fight with rifles, not revolvers. If you will have your post physician dig the slug from the two bodies, I believe you will find they came from a revolver."

"I really don't need it to prove that we have been duped," said Johnston glumly, "but I'll have it done just the same."

Several soldiers carried the two bodies to the infirmary, and the doctor, who was in the crowd, followed them, saying he would dig out the slugs within a few minutes.

Colonel Brett Johnston was feeling sick to his stomach as he thought of Ramino and Zenta, whose bodies still hung on the gallows behind the stable. Sleeving sweat from his brow, he ran his gaze over the crowd and said, "Is Trooper Harry Neal here?"

"Yes, sir!" came the instant reply.

As Neal drew up, Johnston said, "I understand Brondo gave you a message for me before he left you tied up in the guardhouse."

"Yes, sir." Neal nodded. "He said he would get proof that Mr. Smith and Mrs. Wilson were lying about the ambush. He said that you shouldn't kill Ramino and Zenta, that you should hold off until he and Miss Rayva returned. Sir, I told Lieutenant Donovan about Brondo's message, and he said he would give you the message for me. This *is* what he told you, isn't it, sir?"

Johnston held his level gaze on Neal. His words came out ragged. "Lieutenant Donovan told me nothing."

There was a long pause, during which Brondo felt a wordless apprehension. A quick glance at Rayva told him she was experiencing the same feeling.

The colonel turned to Hale Wilson and snapped, "Captain, I want Lieutenant Donovan here on the double!"

Hale Wilson had the complete picture now. Betty and the heavyset redhead had planned this whole ruse to run away together with the payroll money. Half choking on his words, he said, "Donovan isn't in the fort, sir. He's out on special patrol, keeping a watch for Cochise."

As Hale spoke, Brondo leaned inside the stagecoach and produced the two canvas money bags from under one of the seats. Johnston had started to react to Hale's news when he caught sight of the bags. "The payroll!" he gasped.

"Yes, sir," said Brondo, handing the bags to the colonel. "Your two 'victims' hid these in the Rawhide mine."

Johnston swore.

At that moment, the post physician appeared, holding up a lead slug for all to see. "Forty-four caliber, Colonel," he said flatly. "Fired from a revolver at point-blank range. It was not an Apache who killed Lieutenant Simmons."

Brondo glanced at Rayva and then turned to her father. Warily he asked, "Will you release Zenta and Ramino now?"

Colonel Brett Johnston's face took on an ashen pallor, and his eyes remained downcast. For a moment there was a deathly silence. Then with trembling lips he choked out the words, "We . . . we already hanged them."

Rayva gasped, putting her hands to her mouth.

Brondo, his suspicion now confirmed, stared stonily at the colonel. A flame of indignation slowly began to spread through his system. With clipped words he said, "Your Lieutenant Donovan deliberately withheld my message from you, Colonel Johnston. Maybe you are only guilty of mishandling justice . . . but the lieutenant is guilty of murder!"

Johnston's trembling hands were at his temples. Closing his eyes in torment, he whispered, "Yes."

"My father will want vengeance, Colonel," Brondo breathed hotly. "This will mean war!"

Hale Wilson swung a fist through the air in frustration. "How could we have overlooked all this evidence?"

"I can't speak for you, Hale," said Johnston dejectedly, "but I know what it was with me. I was blinded to it by my prejudice toward the Apaches."

Hale swore, shaking his head, and then he held his face in his hands as if unable to believe the truth. The crowd of soldiers looked silently on as he said to Johnston, "My . . .

my wife and Smith murdered the crew and passengers
. . . and scalped them!" He shook his head again. "Then
they hid the money in the mine and shot themselves up a
little to make their story effective."

The colonel was nodding sorrowfully in assent. Speaking
to Lieutenant Clifford Murdock, who stood near, he said,
"Lieutenant, take two men with you to the captain's quarters. Arrest Mrs. Wilson on the charge of murder and put
her in the guardhouse." As Murdock called the names of
two men and walked away, Johnston turned his sick face
toward his captain and sighed, "I'm sorry, Hale."

Hale removed his hat and mopped sweat from his brow
with a red bandanna. "I have to tell you the truth, sir. I'm
not too surprised at this. Don't feel bad. . . . The evidence is conclusive."

The colonel met Rayva's cold glare and looked away.
Turning to the Apache, he said, "Smith left this morning.
We'll go after him once we have tried to pacify your
father. I hope he will accept our apologies. Will you ride
with me to his camp?"

Before Brondo could respond, a guard on the wall sent a
sharp call across the compound, "Colonel! Lieutenant Donovan and his squad are coming on the run—like the devil
himself is after them!"

The gate was swung open, and seconds later the patrol
thundered into the fort, drawing rein in a cloud of dust.
Before his horse had come to a complete stop, Donovan
left the saddle and ran up to Johnston. Short of breath, he
gasped, "Cochise is on his way . . . with at least three
hundred warriors, sir! They're painted up for war!"

Donovan expected the colonel to react with immediate
action. Instead, he saw Johnston stand staring at him with
cold eyes and iron-hard features. Licking his lips, the
lieutenant shifted his gaze toward the crowd of men gathered there. Suddenly he was aware of the bullet-riddled
stagecoach . . . and of the presence of Brondo and Rayva.

Johnston's icy words cut the warm afternoon air. "Harry
Neal gave you a message from Brondo to pass on to me,
Donovan. Why didn't you?"

Brondo stepped close to Donovan, black eyes flashing.

"How did you get Red Smith to lie about me being one of the ambushers, Donovan?"

"What do you mean?" flared Donovan defensively. "Why would I—?"

"To get me hanged so you could claim Rayva for your own!" cut in the angry Apache.

"I don't know what you're talking about," replied Donovan, his mind racing as he attempted to keep his composure.

"Yes, you do," spoke up Rayva. "You tried to get Brondo hanged, just as you tried to get rid of him by leaving him in that shaft at the Rawhide mine."

"What is this all about?" asked the colonel.

"It's true," Rayva said, turning to her father. "The lieutenant and some of his men captured Brondo and tried to prepare an 'accidental' death for him. But Brondo escaped. It was the day that Gary claimed he fell from his horse."

Johnston looked over at Donovan. "Is this true?"

"She's crazy!" Donovan blurted out. "That Apache heathen has filled her head with lies."

Suddenly, a voice called out, "It's the lieutenant who's lying, Colonel." Everyone looked over to where the other members of the patrol were just dismounting and saw Sergeant Harley Carter approaching. "Your daughter is telling the truth," he continued. "I'm ashamed to admit that I was a member of that group."

Johnston turned toward his daughter and Brondo. "Why didn't you tell me—?"

"It would have been the word of an Apache against one of your own officers," Brondo explained.

"There will be a full investigation, and the guilty will be punished," Johnston promised. Then he turned back toward Lieutenant Donovan. "And as for you . . ."

Guilt was evident on the lieutenant's face. He was trapped and he knew it. Suddenly he whipped out his revolver and snapped back the hammer. "Everybody get back!" he growled, inching toward his horse. "I'm leaving, and anybody who tries to stop me gets a bullet in his guts!"

Donovan backed toward his horse but found Sergeant Carter blocking his way.

"You can't do this," Carter said. "It's over."

"The hell it is!" Donovan spat out. "Get out of my way!"

But rather than moving away, Carter lunged for Donovan's gun hand. Swinging the revolver around, the lieutenant fired, the bullet ripping through Carter's chest and knocking him to the ground. Donovan swung the gun back on the others as he continued to his horse and climbed into the saddle. Waving his gun at the crowd, he called to the colonel, "Open up that gate! I'm going out!"

He had just started to wheel his horse when Brondo leaped with the quickness of a cougar. His strong fingers gripped Donovan's pants and shirt, and with one violent jerk, he slammed him to the ground. Donovan landed on his shoulder, and the whole crowd heard bone snap, followed by Donovan's screams of pain as Brondo pounced on him and wrenched the gun from his hand.

"Colonel!" called one of the men at the gate. "Cochise is out there! He's carrying a white flag! I think he wants to talk!"

Johnston barked an order for the sergeant's body to be taken to the infirmary and for Gary Donovan to be placed in the guardhouse, and then he started for the gate. Brondo walked beside him, and they were followed by Rayva and Captain Hale Wilson, along with the rest of the crowd.

Stopping at the gate, they peered out at the painted Apaches. The Indians had fanned out a quarter mile from the fort, sitting their war-striped horses. Cochise was coming in alone, a white flag flapping in the breeze from the tip of his rifle. Behind him Brondo could see Nachise, Naiche, and Geronimo waiting side by side, ready to lead an attack if they were given the signal.

With Rayva now at his side, Brondo said, "Colonel, let me go out and talk to my father first. Maybe I can appease him. I will explain about Ramino and Zenta."

"All right." Johnston nodded.

"Do I have your solemn word that Smith, Mrs. Wilson, and Donovan will pay for their crimes?"

"To the fullest extent of the law," the colonel assured him, speaking through a dry throat.

"What does that mean?"

"They are all guilty of murder. They will hang."

"Even the woman?"

"Even the woman."

"Be ready with your apologies," said Brondo levelly. He squeezed Rayva's hand and strode through the gate.

Johnston sidled up to his daughter, put his arm around her, and said, "Rayva, it may be too late for this, but I must tell you that I am very sorry. If you don't choose to forgive me, I won't blame you."

Rayva said nothing. Her concerned eyes were on the man she loved.

Cochise dismounted, happy to see that his son had not been harmed. As they stood face to face a hundred yards out from the gate, Brondo chose his words carefully. First he told Cochise that Ramino and Zenta had been hanged. The hot-headed chief's initial impulse was to attack the fort immediately, but Brondo calmly restrained him, telling him of Red Stoker's and Betty Wilson's crime. He also told him of Lieutenant Gary Donovan's part in getting the two warriors hanged.

While he held his father's attention, Brondo assured him that the colonel had promised the guilty parties would hang for their deeds.

Skepticism clouded Cochise's eyes. "So Johnston says!" he spat. "More white man's lies!"

"The colonel wants to make his apologies to you, Father," said Brondo, looking back at the silver-haired man in the forefront of the crowd at the gate.

Cochise gripped the rifle in his hands in suppressed fury until the knuckles showed bone white. "I do not want his apologies!" he roared. "I want his *blood*!"

Brondo laid a firm hand on his father's shoulder. "I would have the great Cochise look along the top of the wall."

The chief raised his line of sight to the top of the wall, and his dark eyes immediately widened as he saw the howitzers in firing position. Again he remembered the howitzers at Apache Pass some ten years before.

While Cochise took it in, Brondo said, "Getting more Apaches killed will not bring Zenta and Ramino back,

Father. You can accept Colonel Johnston's apologies and ride away with all three of your sons, or you can order an attack. With the firepower on those walls, it may be that Cochise will be buried today with Nachise, Naiche, and Brondo."

The venerable Chiricahua leader thought on Brondo's words while staring past him at the howitzers. After a long pause, he placed his hand on Brondo's shoulder, just as Brondo's hand still rested on his opposite shoulder. There was love and admiration in Cochise's eyes for this fine, stalwart son. With steady voice, he said, "The Great Spirit has implanted much wisdom within the heart of Cochise's third-born son. Bring the colonel to me."

Brondo felt charged with elation as he turned and waved an arm at the colonel. As Johnston started forward, the men in the fort heaved a sigh of relief. Rayva bit down hard on her lower lip and blinked against the tears that surfaced in her eyes.

While the white men watched from one side and the red men from the other, the two leaders met in the presence of Cochise's third-born son. Brett Johnston gave Cochise his sincere and humble apologies and then guaranteed that Lieutenant Gary Donovan and Betty Wilson would meet swift justice for their crimes, promising that the man known as Red Smith would meet the same fate as soon as he was apprehended. Cochise was invited to attend the hangings if he so desired.

Cochise, accepting the apology and the promise of justice, then asked if he might have the bodies of his two warriors.

After the colonel had turned toward the gate and called for the bodies to be brought forth, he laid a hand on Brondo's shoulder. Setting his gaze on the dark face of Cochise, he said with conviction, "You have a wise and brave son here, Chief. You are to be complimented."

Cochise nodded silently, a light of pride shining in his eyes.

"Are you aware of the relationship that has developed between your son and my daughter?" asked Johnston.

Again the chief nodded silently.

"I want you to know, Cochise," said the colonel, smiling, "that Brondo has my permission to visit Rayva any time he chooses." Johnston then turned to Cochise's son and said, "Brondo, I owe you an apology, also, but I would like to make it in Rayva's presence. Will you step back inside the fort with me?"

After the colonel and Brondo had reentered the fort, the bodies of Zenta and Ramino were brought through the gate, draped over their horses' backs. Cochise stood with them, waiting for Brondo to reappear on his big Appaloosa stallion.

Inside the fort the men dispersed at the colonel's word that there would be no attack from the Apaches. Rayva hurried to Brondo, embracing him, and then stood beside him as her father asked to speak to them.

Faltering, Johnston said, "Rayva . . . I want to tell you again that I am sorry for my foolishness. I . . . I have wronged you, and I have wronged the man you love."

Listening, Rayva began to weep. She wiped away tears with the back of her hand as her father humbly apologized to the handsome young Apache.

"You are forgiven, sir," said Brondo, shaking his hand.

Letting her tears flow, Rayva wrapped her arms around her father and assured him that he had her forgiveness.

When the beautiful half-breed had gained control of her emotions, the colonel said, "One more thing I want to say. I want you two to know that you have my fullest blessings on your relationship."

Brondo shook Johnston's hand again, thanking him, and then turned to the lovely young raven-haired woman. "Rayva," he said tenderly, "I must now ride home with my father. He and I have many things to talk about. I will return in two days."

Rayva stood at the gate of Fort Bowie and watched Brondo and his father ride away, along with three hundred painted Apache warriors. They were almost out of sight when her father moved up beside her. Turning, she looked up into his face.

"That is a magnificent horse, that Appaloosa," he sighed with admiration. "If it wouldn't start a war, I'd steal him."

Rayva looked back toward the Chiricahuas.

Colonel Brett Johnston slipped an arm around his daughter and said with vigor, "That's a magnificent young man, too!"

The next morning Betty Wilson was put on trial and convicted of murder, though she tried to convince everyone present that Red Stoker had done all of the killing. But when it was demonstrated to her in a logical manner that such a thing would have been a physical impossibility, she broke down and admitted the truth, pleading for mercy.

Colonel Brett Johnston eyed Betty coldly as she stood before him in the packed mess hall, flanked by two guards. She wrung her hands as Johnston said, "Mrs. Wilson, you have been proven guilty of murder in this court. You have admitted that you personally murdered Sergeant David McFleary, Lieutenant Donald Simmons, and shotgunner Hector Allen. You have pleaded for mercy. This court believes in justice, Mrs. Wilson. We are going to allow you the same amount of mercy that you gave your victims. Upon the authority invested in me by the U.S. Army, I hereby sentence you to death. You will hang at sunrise tomorrow. Court is adjourned."

Betty Wilson, in the grip of panic, turned and looked at her husband, who sat a few feet away. Terror etched itself on her face as she screamed, "Hale! Help me! *Help me!*"

Hale Wilson gave her a cold, blank stare, and Betty was dragged from the mess hall kicking and screaming.

Everyone remained seated as Gary Donovan was brought in for his trial. He was confronted with the evidence against him, and it was confirmed by trooper Harry Neal's testimony. Donovan was convicted of murdering Sergeant Harley Carter and of conspiracy to send three innocent men to their deaths—Brondo, Zenta, and Ramino. He also was sentenced to hang at sunrise.

At dawn Hale Wilson entered the guardhouse and approached his wife's cell. He noted the irony of the fact that

Gary Donovan was occupying the cell that had held Cochise's third-born son.

Betty was in the cell next to Donovan. She stood at the bars, her hair straggling and her face haggard. Her eyes lit up as her husband came in.

Moving up to the bars, he said impassively, "The guards say you want to see me."

"Yes . . . oh *darling*," she gasped, beginning to weep, "you've got to help me! You can't let them hang me! Please, do something!"

"It's out of my hands," Hale replied coldly.

"No, Hale! You have authority. You're the captain here!" she cried. "I love you, darling! I didn't really mean those things that I said. Please believe me! I love you, Hale. I really do! You've got to save me!"

Eyeing her without emotion, Hale said, "I'm sorry for you, Betty. You've never loved anybody but yourself. Every time you pulled the trigger on those poor innocent people in that stagecoach, you were showing how deeply you love yourself. I'll bet you were planning to do your redheaded boyfriend in, too, so you could have the money all to yourself." With that he turned and walked away.

At the door Hale met the four guards who were coming for the two convicted murderers, and he then walked slowly across the compound toward his quarters. He could hear Betty screaming and wailing as she and Donovan were taken to the gallows. Upon reaching his quarters, he stepped inside, closed the door, and sat down in an over-stuffed chair.

Betty's high-pitched screams were still echoing across the fort. The screaming lasted for another three minutes and then stopped abruptly.

Hale Wilson tried to feel something for her, but it was futile. What he had once felt for her was gone . . . like a bad dream that vanishes with the morning light.

Chapter Fourteen

At midmorning the day after Betty Wilson and Gary Donovan had been hanged, Corporal Ed Shoney knocked on Colonel Brett Johnston's office door.

"Come in!" called Johnston.

Shoney pushed open the door. His eyes fell first on the colonel's stunning daughter, who was seated on a chair in front of her father's desk. "Good morning, Miss Rayva." He smiled.

"Good morning," she echoed.

Rayva was hoping Corporal Shoney would announce that Brondo was there to see her. She was surprised when he looked at her father and said, "Colonel, Chief Cochise is at the gate. He wishes to see you."

Standing up, Johnston said, "By all means show him in, Corporal!"

Rising, Rayva said, "I'll go along home now, Father."

Together they stepped out on the porch of the office building and looked toward the gate. Shoney stepped out on the sun-struck parade grounds and called to the guards, "Send Cochise in!"

The gate swung open, and the venerable Chiricahua leader came riding in on his own mount, leading a frisky Appaloosa stallion colt. When Rayva saw that the colt had the same build and markings as Brondo's horse, her heart leaped to her throat. She stood beside her father as Cochise drew up, and she saw the Indian chief smile for the first time as their eyes met.

Cochise then set his dark eyes on Fort Bowie's commandant and said, "May I dismount, Colonel?"

Johnston's attention was riveted on the beautiful colt. Then swinging his gaze to Cochise, he said, "Of course. Please do."

Rayva remained on the porch as her father moved out into the sunlight and offered Cochise his hand. Men in blue were staring from all over the compound as the two men shook hands. Rayva was still fighting her leaping heart as she heard Cochise say, "Colonel Johnston, this colt is three months old. His sire is Brondo's horse."

"A man would have to be blind not to see that," the colonel said.

Cochise glanced at Rayva and then said to Johnston, "I bring the colt as a gift to you, Colonel. A gift from my son Brondo."

Johnston, flustered, said, "Well, uh . . . why didn't Brondo bring the colt himself?"

Rayva's face flushed. Her heart was racing. Stepping off the porch beside the tall silver-haired man, she said, "Father, don't you know about the Apache custom?"

The puzzled look on the colonel's face showed that he did not.

"Perhaps I should explain," spoke up Cochise. "Colonel, this is the Apache way for a young man to propose to the woman he loves and, at the same time, ask her father for her hand."

Tears were now trickling down Rayva's lovely cheeks.

Johnston cleared his throat and then said, "Please forgive me, Chief, but I'm afraid I am ignorant of your customs." He stood there for a moment, dumbfounded.

"Father," urged Rayva with an elbow in his ribs, "you must tell the chief if Brondo has your consent to have my hand in marriage."

"Oh! Certainly!" he gasped.

With a smile tugging at the corners of his mouth, Cochise handed Johnston the rope that held the colt's halter. "The colt is now yours, Colonel," he said pleasantly.

"You thank your son for me, Chief," said Johnston, "until I get a chance to do so myself. This is one fine horse."

Cochise swung onto the back of his horse. "Brondo would like for the wedding to take place tonight in the Dragoons, where they will live."

"*Tonight?*" gasped the colonel.

"If that meets your approval," answered Cochise.

"Well, this is all pretty sudden, Chief," said Johnston. "I . . . uh . . ." Turning to Rayva, he asked, "Honey, is this all right? I mean, is this too sudden for you?"

"It's not too sudden, Father," she assured him, wiping away her tears. "I love Brondo very, very much. I will gladly become his wife tonight."

"But are you certain you want to live with Brondo's people? You've grown up in our world. Could you adjust?"

"I know it won't be easy, Father, but I must try. I would like to start a school for the Apaches and help them face the future. It is the only hope for peace between my mother's and my father's people."

Colonel Johnston looked at his daughter with a mixture of love and admiration. Then he leaned forward and kissed her warmly on the cheek. Struggling to hold back the tears that were welling in his eyes, he turned to Cochise and said, "It looks like tonight will be the wedding night!"

Smiling broadly, Cochise said, "Brondo is waiting outside the fort. He would like to take his bride with him now, so the Apache women may help her prepare for the ceremony. You and any guests you wish to bring, Colonel, are to appear at the camp at sundown."

Colonel Brett Johnston acknowledged that he would be there. The Chiricahua chief rode out and disappeared through the gate, leaving the colt in the hands of its proud new owner. Moments later Brondo came riding in on his spotted stallion, and the colt nickered.

Rayva ran to Brondo, embracing him as he touched ground. They held on to each other for a moment, locking their eyes. Then looking at her father, Brondo said, "I wish to thank you, Colonel, for giving your consent. I promise that I will love and cherish her till the day I die."

Johnston shook Brondo's hand. "I know you will, son," he responded warmly. "There is no doubt in my mind that the two of you will be very happy together. And I wish to thank you for this fine colt."

Rayva and her father looked at each other and smiled.

"Come," Brondo said to his bride. "We must prepare for the ceremony."

Rayva embraced her father, who again fought tears as she spoke her love for him. Brondo then lifted her up on the Appaloosa's back and swung up behind her. Her eyes were happily tearful as she rode out the gate, sitting in front of Brondo. She heard the colt nicker as the gate closed.

The raven-haired woman sighed as she looked toward the Dragoon Mountains to the west. There she would become the wife of the man she loved—and at that moment she realized that somehow, deep inside, she had always known that her husband would be an Apache.

Brondo could not see it, but a soft, contented smile touched her lips as she cuddled closer to his muscular frame, the magic of love glistening in her dark, expressive eyes.

Epilogue

In that same year of 1872, President Ulysses S. Grant sent General Oliver O. Howard, a one-armed Civil War veteran, to make peace with the Chiricahuas. With the help of an Indian agent named Tom Jeffords, in whom Cochise had confidence, a peace treaty was signed.

The Chiricahuas were allowed to keep their weapons, their way of life, and the land that had been theirs from time immemorial, including the Dragoon and Chiricahua mountains.

Cochise, the foremost Apache enemy of the United States, never again raised a weapon against the whites. Upon signing the treaty, he said, "The white man and the Indian are to drink of the same water, eat of the same bread, and be at peace."

Just two years later, in 1874, the fifty-one-year-old chief took ill and died. On the day of his death, his warriors painted his body yellow, black, and vermilion and shrouded it in a bright red blanket. They propped him up on his horse and took him deep into the mountains.

Somewhere in the Dragoons, the Apaches lowered the body of their revered chief into a lonely grave, the location of which was never revealed.

Cochise's first-born son, Nachise, became chief of the Chiricahuas upon his death. The reign was a brief one. Less than two years later, Nachise died. Naiche, the second son, succeeded to the position of chief of the Chiricahuas in 1876. His rule, however, was not a completely happy one. By popular demand of the people, Naiche had to share his power with Geronimo, who, though a commoner, had a more dynamic personality.

**FROM THE PRODUCER OF WAGONS WEST
AND THE KENT FAMILY CHRONICLES—
A SWEEPING SAGA OF WAR AND HEROISM
AT THE BIRTH OF A NATION.**

THE WHITE INDIAN SERIES

Filled with the glory and adventure of the colonization of America, here is the thrilling saga of the new frontier's boldest hero and his family. Renno, born to white parents but raised by Seneca Indians, becomes a leader in both worlds. THE WHITE INDIAN SERIES chronicles the adventures of Renno, his son Ja-gonh, and his grandson Ghonkaba, from the colonies to Canada, from the South to the turbulent West. Through their struggles to tame a savage continent and their encounters with the powerful men and passionate women in the early battles for America, we witness the events that shaped our future and forged our great heritage.

☐	24650	White Indian #1	$3.95
☐	25020	The Renegade #2	$3.95
☐	24751	War Chief #3	$3.95
☐	24476	The Sachem #4	$3.95
☐	25154	Renno #5	$3.95
☐	25039	Tomahawk #6	$3.95
☐	25589	War Cry #7	$3.95
☐	25202	Ambush #8	$3.95
☐	23986	Seneca #9	$3.95
☐	24492	Cherokee #10	$3.95
☐	24950	Choctaw #11	$3.95
☐	25353	Seminole #12	$3.95
☐	25868	War Drums #13	$3.95

<u>Prices and availability subject to change without notice.</u>